Mr. Budd Novelettes
Stories of Crime and Detection
By
Gerald Verner

Volume One

WILLIAMS & WHITING

Cover design by
Timo Schroeder

9781915887344

Williams & Whiting (Publishers)
15 Chestnut Grove, Hurstpierpoint,
West Sussex, BN6 9SS

CONTENTS

INTRODUCTION

Many of Gerald Verner's stories featured Mr. Robert Budd, a fictional Superintendent of the C.I.D. Scotland Yard. He was a Londoner with his own house at Streatham where he enjoyed growing roses and was sometimes nicknamed The Rosebud. This seemingly sleeping-eyed, ponderous detective had portly, rather obese features. Despite his bulk he could move surprisingly quickly when he needed to and was very shrewd. He could think well and resolved his cases as well as any slick private detective. His rough and ready speech gave him a down-to-earth aspect. He smoked evil smelling thin black cigars and enjoyed a tankard of beer. His abode at Scotland Yard was a small cheerless room. His aide was the melancholy Sergeant Leek, a somewhat slow-witted man who drank lime-juice and soda or lemonade. He unprotestingly bore the brunt of Mr. Budd's caustic criticisms, suffusing this unsettled relationship with humour, as they went about their somewhat unreal, melodramatic, but always entertaining adventures.

*

Green Mask, published by Wright & Brown in August 1934, is the first novel to introduce Mr. Robert Budd and the lugubrious Sergeant Leek at Scotland Yard, and in which Mr. Budd smokes his 'evil smelling thin black cigars'. The origin of *Green Mask* was a Sexton Blake adventure titled *The Fence's Victim*, *Sexton Blake Library No 266* December 1930—de-Blaked by retaining the plot but assigning the Blake role to another character—to become a Superintendent Robert Budd and Sergeant Leek story. *Green Mask* may be the first novel, but it is not the first story to feature the stout detective.

Almost simultaneously with *Green Mask*, *Sinister House* was published by Wright & Brown in 1934, a book made up of

1

three novelettes. *Sinister House* is the title of the first novelette, the second is *Mr. K.*—both stories are reprinted in this first volume—the third novelette was not a Mr. Budd story.

*

Sinister House opens with journalist Anthony Gale, striding along a deserted and dimly-lit road crossing Wimbledon Common. He lives near Putney Heath and often pauses on his way home to look at an empty house from sheer idle curiosity. The house fascinates him:

"Grim and silent, with sightless staring windows, Whispering Beeches stood well back from the roadway, almost hidden in the thickly-growing trees that surrounded it and gave it its name. And its reputation in the neighbourhood was as grim as the house itself, for a tragedy had taken place within that dark and gloomy pile three years previously which had earned it the name of Sinister House."

The above extract from *Sinister House* provides a clue to the true origin of the story. The house is called 'Whispering Beeches' and, circa 1929, Gerald Verner then living and writing as Donald Stuart created a Sexton Blake story, *The Secret of the Whispering Beeches*. It was published in *Union Jack*—a magazine that featured many Sexton Blake stories before coming to an end in 1933 when it was replaced by *Detective Weekly*. However, I can find no firm verifiable record of *The Secret of the Whispering Beeches* as a *Union Jack* story—no cover picture, no date. The only verification for the previous existence of the story is a byline in an Australian newspaper as part of a header for another story, *The Hooded Terror* which ran in the *South Wales Argos* in 1929: 'by Donald Stuart author of *The Invisible Clue, Mister Midnight, The Secret of the Whispering Beeches*," etc...'

Approximately a year later the same story, now with the title *Sinister House* appeared in *The Thriller No.64* April, 1930 also by Donald Stuart priced at 2d. *The Thriller*, was published by Amalgamated Press—a weekly newspaper in circulation from February 1929 to May 1940— that during its eleven-year run published stories by the top thriller writers of the day and built the reputation of others who contributed to its pages. This second version of the story also features Anthony Gale as a journalist. However, the investigating detective was a Superintendent Flower from Scotland Yard, who is called 'Sweet William' by his friends and foes alike, partly because of his name, but mostly because of his passion for flowers of all kinds. He is described as a fat, lethargic and sleepy eyed official. Here unmistakeably is the genesis of Mr. Budd. 'Sweet William' the nickname for Superintendent Flower becomes 'Rosebud' the sobriquet for Mr. Budd, who has a passion for roses. The week before publication, the editor of *The Thriller* wrote in the exaggerated and dramatic PR of the day:

"*Whispering Beeches* otherwise known as *Sinister House*, had more than an evil reputation. Death had stalked abroad, its scythe red with the blood of a murdered man. Since the fatal night when Doctor Shard had been struck down by an unknown hand in his laboratory, the house had remained empty. It was a house of fear; a place that people avoided with cold shudders. There were stories in circulation of shadowy figures seen after nightfall flitting about the weed-choked grounds and of lights flashing behind the dark windows. Such was *Sinister House* when Anthony Gale, journalist, entered it on a voyage of discovery and walked into the grimmest mystery conccivable. A mystery which was beset with tragedy and sudden death."

Wonderful stuff! Following the same story in chronological order, we now come to the version of *Sinister House* published by Wright & Brown in novel form in 1934 featured in this volume. Anthony Gale remains the journalist, but

3

Superintendent Flowers has been replaced by Superintendent Budd. Sergeant Leek does not appear. This is an evolving Mr. Budd who at first smokes cigarettes but graduates to a cigar towards the end of the story, suggesting this may well be the first story to feature the stout superintendent.

The story lives on. In 1936, the same story was republished as *The Terror of Grey Towers* by Donald Stuart in *Detective Weekly No.176* July—a weekly British story paper that ran for 379 issues, from February 25, 1933 to May 25, 1940. No doubt this version was reproduced straight from *The Thriller No.64* April, 1930. The journalist remains Anthony Gale but Mr. Budd has reverted back to Superintendent Flower!

"A mysterious house— A frightened girl— A bewildered man— And behind all— A terrifying unknown menace!"

With changed names of titles and the protagonists, many stories were recycled. Pseudonyms were as common as they were confusing. Republishing *The Thriller* and *Detective Weekly* stories by both Donald Stuart and Gerald Verner as published novels by Wright and Brown was to become the norm, resulting in a complex bibliography, as many of these stories were retitled and locations and the names of the detectives changed. Authors of the day received a one-off fee and took no share in the profits reaped through their work selling in large numbers in England and across the world. They looked to capitalise on their stories as best they could.

*

The second novelette is *Mr. K.*, also a Mr. Budd story without Sargeant Leek. This story originally began life as *The Sinister Quest* by Donald Stuart in *The Thriller No.245* October, 1933 priced at 2d.

"Who wrote the mysterious messages to Scotland Yard which led to the arrest of several 'wanted' men and put the

4

police onto a grim murder in an old country house? Who knew the significance of the sinister green fountain-pen, which seemingly ordinary article led to a trail of danger and death? Was it Mr. 'K' that grim, elusive figure moving always in the background, whose identity was the key problem of *The Sinister Quest?*"

Although *The Sinister Quest* is essentially the same story as *Mr. K.*, the investigating officer in this earlier version is not Mr. Budd either, but Chief Inspector William Flower from Scotland Yard. Notice in this story he is a Chief Inspector not a Superintendent as in *Sinister House, The Thriller No.64* April, 1930. This strongly suggests this story began before Sinister House but where? I have not been able to find any earlier origin but that does not mean it never existed. As Mr. Budd would say: 'It's all very interestin' and peculiar.'

ABOUT THE AUTHOR

Gerald Verner, was born John Robert Stuart Pringle on 31 January 1897 Ramsden Road, Balham - in the Registration District of Wandsworth in the Sub-District of Streatham, London. He was the son of John Charles Rochfort Douglas-Willan Stuart Pringle, a schoolteacher and Ellen Emma Stuart Pringle who performed on the stage as Miss Geraldine Verner. This is the origin of the surname he was later to adopt. At 17, John Robert entered the theatre business as a stage manager for Arthur Bourchier. He remained in the theatre as an acting stage manager until 1921 when that part of his life came to an end.

London was a tough place between the two world wars. Over the next three years he frequently found himself homeless, down-and-out in London, collecting dogends from the gutters, opening them up, and cramming the tobacco into a clay pipe. He turned to producing cabarets in London's leading nightclubs where at the age of 26 he met and married his first wife, Patricia Sayles. When the nightclub boom died, he ended up broke and back on the street.

Nights sleeping rough on the embankment inspired him to write his first detective story *The Clue of the Second Tooth* in pencil on scraps of paper. The story was accepted and when he received £70—less his advance and the cost of typing—he said he had never recaptured the thrill of that moment. It seemed that he had learned to transfer his own bitter experiences of life in the raw to an enthralled audience hungry for detective fiction. The story appeared in the *Sexton Blake Library No 105*, on 31 August 1927, but as anonymous. Amalgamated Press did not credit any authors until June 1930.

Donald Stuart began writing regularly for *The Sexton Blake Library*. Hungry to capitalise on the new career opportunity that had opened for him he wrote a total of 44 stories. His style was heavily influenced by that of Edgar Wallace. He adopted the name Donald Stuart and not just writing as Donald Stuart; he became Donald Stuart. He opened a bank account in the name of Donald Stuart and brought the shutters down on his old life as Pringle. In the 1930s Donald Stuart wrote 4 stories for the magazine *Union Jack*, 3 for *The Thriller* and 7 for *Detective Weekly*. With changed names of titles and the protagonists, many of these stories were recycled. He wrote six novels for the publisher Wright & Brown; *The White Friar* in 1934, followed by *The Man Outside*, and *The Shadow*, all published in the same year. *The Man in The Dark*, *The Valley of Terror*, and *Midnight Murder*, followed in 1935.

During 1928, Donald Stuart wrote his first stage play, no doubt harking back to his theatrical roots. It was called *The Shadow* and was a comedy thriller, produced by Mr. Nicholas Hannen at the Embassy Theatre in London. It featured distinguished comedian Bert Coote and his company. *The Shadow* was made into a film in 1933. It was published as a novel by Wright & Brown in 1934 and rewritten as *Danger at Westways* for the *Sexton Blake Library*, number 645, in November 1938.

In June 1930, he ambitiously formed his own production company Donald Stuart Productions Limited, to produce *Sexton Blake*, a bold detective melodrama with elaborate and expensive stage effects, including a bomb explosion, and a car smashing into a train at a level crossing. The production also featured an abduction in a real taxicab driving down Baker Street followed by a real motorcycle. There were three dress rehearsals to get all this technically right on the night. Taxi drivers were invited to the first dress rehearsal, detectives from Scotland Yard were invited to the second. The production never recouped its costs.

In an attempt to bury misfortune and start over Donald Stuart was relegated to the wings and, though he continued to write occasionally as Donald Stuart, he borrowing from his mother's stage surname, and Gerald Verner took centre stage.

As Gerald Verner he wrote in parallel with Donald Stuart for *The Thriller, Detective Weekly, Thriller Library, Thrilling Detective*, and *The Boy's Friend-Bulls Eye Library*. He began writing hardbacks for Wright & Brown, most of which began life as stories for *The Sexton Blake Library*. His output became so prolific that to avoid saturating the market with books under the Gerald Verner banner, he sought a second publisher—there was obviously a limit on just how many books Wright & Brown could accept in one year—The Modern Publishing Company at 6 Farringdon Avenue, London E.C.4., for whom he wrote five novels under the pseudonym Derwent Steele and another five under the pseudonym Nigel Vane, with an additional Nigel Vane story *The Midnight Men* for publishers Stanley Smith 59, New Oxford Street W.C.1.

Gerald Verner's first book for Wright & Brown, 12-14 Red Lion Court, Fleet Street, London E.C.4, *The Embankment Murder* was published in 1933. Originally a *Sexton Blake Library* story by Donald Stuart called *The Clue of the Second Tooth*. This debut novel was swiftly followed by *Alias the Ghost, The Black Hunchback, Black Skull, The Death Play, Phantom Hollow*, and *The Next to Die*. Many authors sold their stories on to Wright & Brown, following publication in magazine form or newspaper serialisations to take advantage of the lending libraries, their main outlet. As the lending libraries declined after the war Wright & Brown declined with them eventually going into voluntary liquidation at the close of 1969 leaving no debt and having lost money for several years.

May 1935 saw an announcement in *The Bookseller* that The Prince of Wales has honoured a detective story writer, Gerald Verner, by graciously accepting a special Jubilee edition of fifteen of his novels. The set has been printed on special paper and bound in Jubilee blue with gilt lettering on the spine.

By 1936 at the age of 40, a veritable one-man factory of crime fiction, Gerald Verner was one of the most successful crime writers in the country having sold some one and a half million copies of his stories and having written 23 novels in five years as well as nearly 100 short stories, serials and plays. Like Edgar Wallace, he used to dictate his novels into a dictaphone.

1932 to the outbreak of the Second World War were Gerald Verner's golden years of writing detective fiction. He was very popular. His novels were translated into over 35 languages, selling in hundreds of thousands in Great Britain, Australia, New Zealand, Canada, and in the USA published by Macaulay Company, New York. They were translated into Polish, Hungarian, Norwegian, French, Dutch, and in Germany by Eden-Verlag, Berlin. Stories were serialised across the world, like *The Silver Horseshoe* in *The Australian Women's Weekly*. He also used to edit the quarterly magazine *Crime*.

Favourite detectives were Trevor Lowe—backed up by his assistant Arnold White— who featured in fourteen books, and Mr. Robert Budd, a fictional Superintendent of the C.I.D. Scotland Yard—with the melancholy Sergeant Leek—who featured in twenty-seven.

In July 1946, Gerald Verner married Isobel Ronald, in the registration district of North Eastern Surrey. Isobel was a war widow with two sons, Anthony James Ronald and James Jack Ronald. Their father was Jack Ronald, killed at El Alamein in 1942, and the adopted son of another famous and talented writer, James Ronald. The wedding records have entered both his names Gerald Verner and John R. S. Pringle. They took a coach trip to Switzerland as a honeymoon. In December 1949 they had a son, Christopher.

The war drew a line under this golden age of detective fiction and authors were forced to turn to radio and then to television for work. Gerald Verner began writing for radio, three eight-part radio serials, beginning with *The Tipster* in April 1948, followed by *The Show Must Go On* in August the same year. *The Show Must Go On* was subsequently turned into a book for Wright & Brown in 1950, and was made into a film in 1952 called *Tread Softly*, directed by David Macdonald and made by Albany Films. *Noose for a Lady* was broadcast in July 1950, and was made into a 73 min film in 1953 by Insignia Films Directed by Wolf Rilla. In 1992 the BFI initiated a search for some of the best lost British films. As part of this effort, they published a book *Missing Believed Lost* which listed and described 92 of the most sought-after films. *Noose for a Lady* is on that list. It has now been found and issued on DVD.

Slim Callaghan, a fictional British private detective in the American hard-boiled mode, was the central character in several popular Peter Cheyney novels including *The Urgent Hangman* and *Dangerous Curves*. From the book *The Urgent Hangman* Gerald Verner adapted a stage play called *Meet Mr. Callaghan* which opened May 1952 at the Garrick Theatre, London. The stage adaptation of *Meet Mr. Callaghan* was made into a film in 1954 by Eros Films Limited.

July 31st, 1956, saw his television serial play in seven episodes *The Crimson Ramblers* begin on London (Channel 9). Directed by Robert Evans, it had the distinction of being the first thriller serial on ITV. That same year, on the 4th September, Agatha Christie's *Towards Zero* opened at the St James's Theatre, London, dramatised by her and Gerald Verner. That year also heralded *Sorcerer's House* for publishers Hutchinson, the sequel to *Noose for a Lady*, the first novel to feature amateur sleuth Simon Gale.

Following the successful publication of *Sorcerer's House*, Gerald Verner began a follow-up third Simon Gale story to be titled, *The Snark Was A Boojum*. Its forthcoming publication was announced in the press, but unfortunately, this intriguing opus was never completed in his lifetime. It was to be in three parts, but he never completed part three. The reason was a messy divorce which had a bad effect upon his health preventing him from writing anything. In 2015, his son Chris Verner managed to complete the story and it was published by Ramble House, Vancleave, Mississippi that same year.

During April 1961, Gerald Verner had a meeting with Ian Hendry and Patrick Macnee to discuss scripts for a forthcoming TV series to be called *The Avengers*. He wrote Episode 18 called *Double Danger*, transmitted on Southern Television, Saturday 8 July 1961, directed by Roger Jenkins and produced by Leonard White.

In 1960 he continued writing again for Wight & Brown with a novel version of his TV serial *The Crimson Ramblers*, though with the slow death of the lending libraries, business was not as before. Seventeen books followed right up to 1967, some of them rewrites, when he switched back to Donald Stuart, to write 17 x 30 min *Sexton Blake Case Histories* for B.B.C. Radio, broadcast from August – December, starring William Franklyn as Sexton Blake.

Gerald Verner died of natural causes at Broadstairs, Kent, on 16th September, 1980. Following his death, his fiction slipped out of print, but the last decade has seen an astonishing revival of his books on both sides of the Atlantic.

Chris Verner
Berkhamsted
April 2023

SINISTER HOUSE

CHAPTER 1

The Empty House

Psychologists have stated that the human brain is incapable of holding two troubles at the same time and giving an equal amount of attention to each. The greater worry will invariably overcome the lesser, and Anthony Gale, as he strode savagely along the deserted and dimly-lighted road crossing Wimbledon Common, would have been the first to admit the truth of this—if he had thought about it at all, which he did not. His mind was far too fully occupied with his recent quarrel with Mollie to allow room for profound truths to creep in, and he was also in a very bad temper, which is not the ideal state for any man who wishes to indulge in sane and consecutive thought.

So angry was he that for the first time during the past three weeks he had totally forgotten the fact that he was out of work and with no immediate prospect of finding a job, the opportunities offered to little-known freelance journalists with a predilection for crime stories being few and far between. Women were unreasonable, thoroughly unreasonable, he thought angrily. After all, he had only asked Mollie a simple question. There was no need for her to have flown into a temper, and what had she been doing, anyway, on the previous evening with Louis Savini in Shaftesbury Avenue?

Anthony disapproved of Savini. Any decent fellow would disapprove of a man who was known to be a crook and a blackmailer and something worse, associating with the girl to whom he was practically engaged. Besides, Mollie had deliberately lied to him. He had gone to considerable trouble in getting two seats for the new show at the Orpheum because she had said she wanted to see it—luckily the manager was a friend of his; funds did not permit of his buying expensive theatre tickets—and at the last moment, just as he had been preparing to dress, she had phoned up to say that she'd got such a bad headache that she was going to bed, and would he excuse her?

Anthony had been duly sympathetic—he remembered bitterly some of the extravagant things he had said—and had spent a most boring evening sitting beside an empty seat watching one of the worst plays he had ever seen. It was only the fact that the seats had been given to him that had prevented his walking out after the first act.

It had been purely an accident that he had seen Mollie at all. There had been a traffic block, and while he was waiting to cross the street to catch his bus she had come out of the Trocadero, looking radiantly beautiful in a new evening dress, and accompanied by—Anthony ground his teeth—Louis Savini! They had got into a waiting taxi and driven off before he had had time to recover from his first shock of surprise.

After spending a wakeful night and considerably more tuppences than he could afford in trying to ring the girl up, Anthony had hurried round to her flat at the first available opportunity, only to be told that she was out.

Cooling one's heels for over five hours and a half on the corner of a busy street is not the ideal method by which to prepare for a delicate interview, and Anthony felt the strain.

He communicated some of this in his manner when he did eventually meet the girl, and his greeting, if not exactly cold, was certainly lacking in that carefree joyousness which Mollie appeared to expect. His subsequent remarks too, were the reverse of tactful. There were several things he called Savini without once mentioning the word 'gentleman', and Mollie retaliated—with her own private opinion of men in general and Anthony in particular, concluding with a fervent wish that she might never see him again, and following this up with a strategic movement that left him gazing stupidly at the polished front door that had just been slammed in his face.

All these things considered Anthony felt, as he walked homeward with long angry strides, that he had just cause for thinking that women were unreasonable. There was, too, a dull heavy ache somewhere inside him, and art insane longing to get out of himself so that he could not think, that was anything but pleasant. What could there be in common between a girl like Mollie Trayne and an oily crook of Savani's calibre? he wondered miserably. Until chance had opened his eyes, he had never even known that they were acquainted, and Mollie had flatly refused to offer any explanation for her inexplicable behaviour.

Anthony strode on savagely, kicking at the loose stones on the surface of the rough road, his brain dizzy and aching from the chaotic whirl that revolved ceaselessly about one central, fixed idea. Mollie had turned him down for a slimy creature in whose veins was such a mixture of nationalities that it would have been impossible to extradite him without dividing him into four quarters! Anthony at that moment would have cheerfully undertaken such a congenial task. He was conscious of a horrible sense of blankness—or something terribly vital to his existence that had been destroyed, and deep within him a hopelessness that was almost unbearable.

He lived in a tiny cottage on the outskirts of Roehampton, and there was no necessity for him to have come this roundabout way home, except that he felt he wanted exercise and a longing for space and air. The cottage was his own freehold—it had been left him, together with a small legacy, by an aunt two years before—and that was Anthony's only excuse for living so far off the beaten track.

He came eventually to the end of the common, crossed over a broad road and struck off again, skirting the corner of Putney Heath. His sense of direction was entirely mechanical, but he was well acquainted with every inch of the neighbourhood and could have found his way blindfold.

17

Presently he swung into a wide avenue that led through to within a hundred yards of his small demesne. It was lined on either side by large houses, each standing in its own considerable acreage of ground. Most of them, as Anthony knew well, were empty and neglected, relics of a past prosperity awaiting demolition by the jerry-builders and the erection of 'Modern desirable residences' in their stead.

There was one house, about halfway down the avenue that had always interested him because of the history that attached to it. Grim and silent, with sightless staring windows, Whispering Beeches stood well back from the roadway, almost hidden in the thickly-growing trees that surrounded it and gave it its name. And its reputation in the neighbourhood was as grim as the house itself, for a tragedy had taken place within that dark and gloomy pile three years previously which had earned it the name of Sinister House. The figure of Death had stalked abroad there, its scythe red with the blood of a murdered man. Since the fatal night when Doctor Shard had been struck down by an unknown hand in his laboratory, the house had remained empty, and had the reputation of being haunted.

There were stories in circulation of shadowy figures seen after nightfall flitting about the weed-choked grounds and of lights flashing behind the dark windows.

Anthony believed none of these stories, but from sheer idle curiosity and because the place fascinated him, he had made a habit of stopping every time he passed the house at nightfall and looking at its black bulk, dimly visible at the end of the long drive. He had never seen anything, but it had become almost second nature with him, and tonight, although his mind was elsewhere, the habit asserted itself and be paused for a second by the broken gate. Almost unconsciously he surveyed the house and as he looked, he suddenly drew in his breath with a sharp hiss.

In one of the lower rooms a light gleamed! Anthony Gale concluded that his imagination was playing tricks with him. He closed his eyes quickly and opened them again, expecting to find that he had made a mistake, and that the house would be in darkness. But the light was still there, faint and dim like a will-o'-the-wisp. Then, as he continued to gaze steadily at the window from which it came, a dark something passed in front of it, and an instant later it went out!

All the journalist in Anthony came uppermost. For a moment he forgot his quarrel with Mollie, forgot everything except that he had stumbled on the possibility of a 'story'. Without hesitation he began to make his way up the dark drive, avoiding the gravel and keeping to the grass borders. Long neglected by shears and mower it was thick and rank and completely deadened his footsteps so that he advanced noiselessly to where a huge yew tree grew in front of the main entrance. In the shadow of the massive trunk, Anthony paused and listened.

The night was very still and, save for the faint rustic of the leaves as the topmost branches of the beech trees stirred softly in the faint breeze, there was not a sound. What was the explanation of that light? Obviously, there was someone about in that deserted house and Anthony was determined to find out who and what they were doing.

He crept forward stealthily until he reached the steps leading up to the shadowy porch. Here he saw something that the darkness had prevented him from seeing before. The front door was open! He felt a thrill of excitement run through his veins. Who was inside and why?

Without a sound he tip-toed up the worn, moss-grown steps and noiselessly entered the pitch-black hall, pausing again to listen as he crossed the threshold. This time he thought he detected a slight sound, an almost inaudible sibilant sigh that seemed to come from somewhere on his right.

Anthony felt the hair on the back of his neck prickle. There was something altogether horrible about that sigh from the darkness. He waited motionless and rigid, but there was no repetition of the sound, and after a minute he began to move forward slowly. The room in which the light had been was on the right of the front door, and he stretched out his hand and felt along the wall on that side of the hall, until presently his groping fingers came in contact with the frame of a door. He felt round this and touched nothing but empty air. The door was apparently open.

Anthony advanced cautiously, and as he did so an overpowering sense of being watched took possession of him. The presence as of somebody behind him—out in the black vastness of the hall! He took two more steps forward, and almost cried out as he stumbled over something that lay on the floor—something that was soft and yielding! He put out both hands instinctively to save himself, fell on his knees, and touched something wet and sticky!

With a sharp cry of horror, he recoiled and, pulling out a box of matches from his pocket, struck a light. In the feeble yellow glimmer, he saw that he had fallen over the body of a man—a man who lay stark and rigid with a gaping wound in his throat. But it was the white, terror-distorted features that held Anthony's gaze. For it was the face of Louis Savini!

CHAPTER 2

The Man in the Dark!

Louis Savini!

There was no mistaking that dark, sallow face, in spite of the fact that the thick, over-red lips were twisted back in a grin of agony and terror.

Anthony felt a curious, cold sensation creep down his spine as the match he was holding flared up suddenly and died down, and at the same time from behind came the faint creak of a disturbed floorboard, the almost inaudible shuffle of a step! He remembered the feeling of an unseen presence and swung round, the dying match burning his fingers. A figure, black, shapeless, was creeping towards him from the open door! A crouching deformed-looking shape, with two white, talon-like hands, outstretched, crooked and clutching before it! Anthony felt a wave of terror, such as he had never experienced before, steal over him at the sight of those long, slim, ivory hands, and then the match went out!

The blackness after even that feeble glimmer was intense, and the silence that followed indescribably horrible. It seemed as if the whole universe suddenly stood still, and then out of the darkness came a rustle, the faint swirl of silk-like garments, and the next second something launched itself at Anthony, and he was fighting desperately to keep those bony fingers from his throat!

A shudder went through him as the clawing hands of his unknown adversary touched the skin of his face and neck, for they were cold with the coldness of something long since dead; the uncanny chill of death itself! And yet behind their grip was an enormous strength, a strength that taxed his muscles to the utmost as he strained to free himself from that strangling grasp. One skinny hand had fastened on his throat and the twining

21

fingers were tightening, tightening, causing the blood to thunder to his brain.

Exerting all his force, Anthony wrenched madly at a thin, steel-like wrist, but without avail. The hold about his neck never loosened the fraction of an inch. Great purple and orange lights flashed before his eyes, and he felt his senses reeling. A few more seconds and he knew that he would lose consciousness. With a supreme effort he succeeded in freeing his right hand from the clutch of the other and struck out blindly. He heard a faint gasp of pain, and for an instant the choking grip relaxed. He staggered back two paces, drawing in great gulps of air hoarsely and painfully, tripped over the body of the dead man, and fell heavily to the floor. Before he could even attempt to struggle to his feet, his unseen assailant was on him, and again he felt those horrible hands seeking for his throat. If once they got a second grip, Anthony knew that he was done for. Grasping the fleshless wrists of his attacker, he strove to keep those eager fingers away from his neck, but slowly and surely the other gained ground.

Anthony's aching muscles cracked under the strain, but his arms were being gradually forced up. The unknown man in the dark seemed possessed of almost inhuman strength. Anthony could feel his hot breath fanning his cheek, but no sound escaped him, and there was something horrible, uncanny in that very fact, that silent remorseless struggle for mastery.

At last, with a shock that sent a convulsive movement through his limbs, he felt the icy touch of those death-like fingers on his chin; another moment and they would be at his throat! With a sudden jerk he twisted his body to one side, still grimly holding on to the other's wrists. Over and over, they rolled across the floor, and eventually Anthony found himself uppermost. His advantage, however, was short-lived, for his opponent was as slippery as an eel. Wrenching his hands free, he suddenly gripped Anthony round the back of his neck, at the same time thrusting both his knees upwards sharply. Anthony turned a complete somersault over the other's head and landed with a crash on his back. His head struck the floor with terrific force, and to the accompaniment of myriads darting lights he lost consciousness!

*   *   *   *

His first impression, as his senses slowly returned to him, was that his usually comfortable bed had, in some manner, developed an unaccustomed hardness. Every bone in his body ached and his temples seemed to contain an imprisoned steam-hammer that was trying its utmost to burst a way through his brain. With a groan, he pressed his hands to his forehead and sat up. The movement caused the agonizing pain in his head to increase, but after a moment this abated slightly.

He was in pitch darkness, except for a dim square of dark blue to his right, and as his mind gradually cleared, he remembered his discovery of the dead body of Savini and his fight with the unknown man in the dark. Apparently, he was still in the empty house. After waiting for a moment to let the pain in his temples subside, Anthony struggled shakily to his feet, feeling in his pockets for his matches. They were not there, and he remembered having dropped the box at his shock on first discovering Savini. He felt about on the floor and presently found them. The box had been crushed under foot during the struggle and its contents scattered, but, luckily, it still held three matches. Anthony struck one and, as it flared into life, looked about him. He failed to suppress the involuntary cry of amazement that escaped him when his eyes went to the spot where the dead man had been, for—the body of Louis Savini had vanished!

Anthony stared stupidly at the bare floor unable to believe his own eyes. Surely, he could not have imagined the whole thing? His fingers strayed to his throat tenderly. He certainly hadn't imagined the fight in the dark—the pain in his head and the soreness of his neck were proofs enough that that had been no dream creation! The match in his fingers went out and he struck another, bending down to examine the floor. No, there was no room for doubt. There, on the bare boards, was a large, sinister, irregular stain. He looked at his hands. They too were bloodstained. Savini had been murdered, but for some reason his body had been removed while Anthony had been unconscious.

He struck his third match and, looking round the bare room, saw an end of candle stuck on the corner of the marble mantelpiece. It must have been the light from that, he concluded, that had at first attracted his attention. He went over and lighted it. As he did so, he saw propped up against the wall behind it an envelope. Some writing was scrawled across it in pencil and, bending nearer as the candlelight grew stronger, Anthony, with something akin to a shock, made out his own name! The writer evidently knew him!

He tore open the flap and extracted the contents, a single sheet of cheap notepaper. Written on it, in the same sprawling hand as the address on the envelope, was the following:

'You will be sensible if you forget everything that you have seen tonight. I could have killed you as easily as I killed Savini and shall not hesitate to do so if you become a nuisance. You escaped with your life merely because you know nothing. Where ignorance is—life, it is folly to be wise.'

That was all. There was no signature. Anthony pursed up his lips in a silent whistle as he put the warning in his pocket, thoughtfully. He had stumbled into a veritable maze of mystery. What a 'story'! A front-page story with 'banner' headlines:

'MIDNIGHT MURDER IN EMPTY HOUSE!
HISTORY REPEATS ITSELF IN SINISTER MANSION
AT ROEHAMPTON.'

There was not a news editor in Fleet Street who would not welcome him with open arms, it was a big 'scoop'. The biggest that had ever come his way. Anthony made up his mind to take it to the *Courier*. He had done several odd jobs for Downer, and he might possibly get a commission to 'cover' the affair. He glanced at his watch. It was half-past one. If he hurried straight away and was lucky enough to get hold of a taxi, he would be in time to do a write-up for the morning edition. They'd hold up the presses for a story like this—an exclusive.

He took a hasty look round the bare and dilapidated room to see if there was anything that would give him a clue to the identity of the man who had attacked him—the murderer of Savini. But there was nothing and, picking up the end of candle, he turned to depart. Making his way out into the wide hall, he was about to open the front door, which was now closed, when a faint sound from the shadows of the big staircase startled him and made him swing round hurriedly.

A dark heap of something lay at the foot of one of the massive banisters and, as he looked, it stirred slightly, and a smothered moan reached his ears. Holding the candle above his head, Anthony approached cautiously and bent down.

And here he received the third and greatest shock of that night of surprises, for the dark heap was revealed as the figure of a woman, and the wide eyes that stared up at him from the ashen face were the wide eyes of Mollie Trayne!

CHAPTER 3

The Night Intruder

Anthony hastily stuck the candle on the ledge of the lower stair and dropped on his knees beside the girl.

"Mollie!" he exclaimed, blank astonishment in his voice. "What on earth are you doing here?"

She looked at him vacantly for a moment, her eyes dull and lustreless. Then she struggled up on his supporting arm. A faint whiff came to his nostrils as she moved, a sickly-sweet smell that left no doubt in his mind as to the cause of her present state. The girl was recovering from the effects of a drug. She had been chloroformed!

"Tony!" She breathed the name almost inaudibly, "Tony, what happened? I—I feel dreadfully sick!" Her voice trailed on incoherently.

"You'll feel worse if you try to move," he replied, as she made an effort to rise. "Lie still for a moment and the sickness will pass off."

She sank back against his arm and passed a trembling hand over her eyes. For a few moments she lay motionless, with closed lids, while Anthony watched her anxiously, puzzling his brains as to the meaning of this fresh development. What was Mollie doing at this sinister house at that hour of the morning? Evidently, she had been attacked by the same mysterious person who had fought with him in the dark, but what had brought her there in the first place? Had she come with Savini? Anthony went cold at the thought. If she had, unless she had been drugged beforehand, she must have been a witness to the murder!

Presently she opened her eyes and he saw that they had recovered something of their brightness.

"Feel better now?" he asked gently, and she nodded.

26

"Yes, thank you," she replied.

"Tell me what happened," said Anthony, helping her sit up.

"I don't know," she answered. "I only remember getting as far as the front door, and then somebody caught me by the shoulders and before I could move or cry out something was pressed over my face, and I don't remember any more."

"But what brought you here? Why did you come?" demanded Anthony.

Mollie rose unsteadily to her feet clutching at his arm for support.

"I—I can't tell you that," she said in a low shaky voice," and swayed so badly Anthony had to slip his arm round her waist to keep her from falling.

"You'd better sit down again for a moment," he advised, and tried to lead her over to the stairs, but Mollie shook her head.

"No, no," she whispered, glancing around her with terrified eyes, "Let me get away from this horrible place. It frightens me!"

She made a faltering step towards the door.

"So, you won't tell me what you came here for?" he persisted,

"I can't," she repeated, and her voice sounded stronger and held a note of finality in it.

"Did you come with Savini?" asked Anthony sharply and felt her fingers tighten on his arm at the question.

"No," she replied slowly, "I didn't come with Mr. Savini."

"I suppose," went on Anthony sarcastically, "that you had no idea he was here?"

"Yes!" She breathed the words so softly that he could scarcely catch what she said. "Yes, I knew that he was here!"

"And that was the reason you came?"

"Partly." The answer was a long time coming, as though it were being forced out of her against her will.

27

"I see," said Anthony bitterly; "you needn't trouble to explain any further."

"You don't see!" she cried sharply. "You don't see at all!"

"I think I do," he retorted, and then with that odd unaccountable desire which comes to people to hurt the ones they love most, he added: "Anyway, you'll never be able to meet Savini again. He's dead!"

"Dead!" she gasped. "Not—not murdered?"

A wave of contrition for the unnecessary bluntness of his remark swept over Anthony.

"I'm sorry," he muttered; "I shouldn't have told you like that. I—"

"But you must—you must tell me!" she interrupted, grasping the lapels of his coat with both hands. "You must tell me everything! How did it happen? Where?"

He remained silent, wondering why she had jumped so quickly to the conclusion that it had been murder.

She waited a moment and then, as he did not reply, she continued in a husky whisper:

"Was it—here?"

Anthony nodded.

"Murdered!" She looked fearfully about her with terror in her eyes, as she murmured the ominous word.

"I didn't say he was murdered," said Anthony watching her covertly, "I only said he was dead."

She raised her eyes to his face inquiringly, but it was in shadow, and she could see nothing of its expression.

"Wasn't he—" she stopped, leaving the sentence unfinished.

"He was, as a matter of fact," Anthony admitted. "But what made you think so?"

"I—I don't know—I just thought—" she stammered vaguely and the hand on his arm trembled violently. Then suddenly she burst out: "Oh, let us go-—let us go!"

She ran to the door and began to fumble with the latch desperately, glancing back over her shoulder with wide eyes.

Anthony followed, carrying the end of the candle in his hand and, as he passed the open door of the room where Savini had met his death, his foot kicked against some small object that lay on the floor. He stooped quickly and picked it up. It was a little leather case and, without waiting to give it more than a cursory glance, he hastily slipped it into his pocket. Mollie's attention had been taken up with the fastenings of the front door and she had failed to notice his action.

As he reached her side, she managed to twist back the catch and stepped out into the darkness of the porch.

"If we can find a taxi, I'll take you home," he said, as she hurried down the steps and half-walking, halt-running, made her way quickly along the weed-grown drive.

"You needn't bother—I've got a car," she answered breathlessly,

"Got a car!" he echoed in astonishment.

"Yes, I left it round the corner—in a side street."

Anthony flung away the still lighted end of candle that he had been carrying and gripped her arm.

"Look here, Mollie!" he exclaimed sternly. "You're hiding something. What do you know about this business?"

She did not attempt to pull away from him or even deny his statement but remained silent.

"You must have come here for some reason," he continued. "What was it?"

"It's no good asking me, Tony," she said after further silence, and there was a hint of impatience in her voice. "I've said once that I can't tell you, and I mean it."

"But—" he began, and she interrupted him.

"You don't understand, and it's better that you shouldn't try," she spoke rapidly and nervously. "Forget all about tonight, and what happened in that horrible house as quickly as you can.

It's got nothing to do with you, and you'll be wise if you take my advice."

They had reached the gate by now and, passing through, she stopped on the pavement.

"Ring me up tomorrow—in the afternoon," she went on. "And remember what I've said." She squeezed his arm and, before he could speak or stop her, was running swiftly down the deserted avenue.

For a moment Anthony felt inclined to follow her and demand an explanation of her strange words, and then realizing the futility of it, shrugged his shoulders and looked undecidedly about him. A clock somewhere in the distance struck two sonorous strokes and warned him of the lateness of the hour. Even if he were lucky enough to pick up a belated cab, which was extremely unlikely, it would be useless going to the offices of the *Courier* now. He wouldn't get there until nearly three if he started at once, and by the time he had written his 'copy' it would be too late anyway for the morning editions.

He made up his mind to go home and see Downer first thing in the morning, and with this intention turned and swung off in the opposite direction to that taken by Mollie, covering the ground at a good pace.

He occupied the short walk to his cottage in reviewing the mysterious events of the evening and trying vainly to account for Mollie's extraordinary behaviour, and the reasons for her presence at Whispering Beeches. The whole thing, from the murder of Louis Savini onwards, was inexplicable—a nightmare—and Anthony felt his tired brain reel dizzily as he tried to grapple with it. He arrived at his cottage, let himself in and, switching on the light in the tiny dining room, mixed himself a stiff whisky-and-soda and drank it at a gulp.

His aimless wanderings of the evening and the excitement that had followed had made him feel dead tired and he was in his bedroom and partly undressed before he remembered with a start the little leather case he had picked up in the hall of the empty house.

Reaching over for his jacket, he took it from his pocket. It was a flat pouch-like affair of pliable leather, fastened with a catch button and remarkably old. There was something hard inside, and Anthony knew it was a key before he put in his finger and took it out, with a slip of paper.

The key had obviously been made to fit a patent lock, for it was shaped something like a Yale, though only half the size. Anthony examined the paper that had accompanied it. It bore several jumbled lines of letters and figures and was evidently either a code or the key to a code. The paper was old; the lettering in ink that had already begun to fade.

Anthony searched the case carefully for a further clue, but there was none, nor did it bear any markings. He decided to examine it more closely in the morning and replacing the key and the paper slipped it under his mattress and with a weary yawn continued his undressing. His head had hardly touched the pillow before he was asleep.

A faint sound from somewhere near at hand woke him instantly and he sat up in bed. The room was in darkness but outside the door and immediately opposite was a landing window, which overlooked the little garden at the back, and there was enough light in the sky to show him that his door was opening slowly! He watched, listening intently, and presently heard somebody breathing softly. The door swung wider and now he could see silhouetted dimly against the grey square of the window beyond, the vague shadowy figure that was stealthily entering!

Anthony silently stretched out his hand towards a small electric torch he kept on the table beside his bed and, without removing his eyes from that sinister creeping shape, closed his fingers round it. A loose board creaked and, at the sound, Anthony sprang out of bed and flashed on his lamp.

He caught a glimpse of a black figure crouched to spring; saw the lowered head enveloped in a bag-like mask, and then something struck him on the shoulder so violently that he dropped the torch and in another second was grappling with the intruder.

His right hand touched something cold, and he felt a sharp pain shoot up his arm and his fingers became wet and sticky. He guessed that it was a knife that the night visitant carried and lashed out wildly. He heard a smothered gasp and a clatter as something fell to the floor, received a kick on the shin that sent him stumbling to his knees, and then a door slammed, and the key turned in the lock.

Anthony staggered to his feet and limping across to the light switch pressed it down. The room was empty. The intruder had gone, leaving behind him as a souvenir of his presence the long-bladed, black-handled knife that glittered evilly on the floor!

Anthony had to break open the door before he could make his way to the bathroom and bathe and bandage the deep cut on the back of his hand, which was bleeding profusely. It was during this operation that he suddenly realized the object of the burglary. The visitor of the night had been seeking the leather wallet that he had picked up in the hall of the empty house!

CHAPTER 4

The Green Car

All desire for further sleep had left him and having attended to his wound, Anthony made his way downstairs. The first pale streaks of dawn were filtering in through the windows of the dining room and, glancing at the clock on the mantelpiece, he saw that it was half-past four. He also saw something else. The drawers of the sideboard had been pulled out and their contents scattered in a heap on the carpet.

With a grim little smile tightening the corners of his mouth Anthony explored further and found, as he had expected, that every room in the cottage had been subjected to a methodical and rigorous search. Evidently the intruder had exhausted all other possibilities before turning his attention to the bedroom, for even the kitchen and the hallstand had not escaped him.

His means of gaining admittance had been through a window in the microscopic scullery, for Anthony found the neat circle of glass that had been cut out to enable his hand to raise the catch, lying on the sill. Whatever secret the key and the slip of paper contained it was obviously of considerable value to the unknown person or persons behind this mysterious business. Anthony examined his rifled home carefully to see if he could find any clue to the identity of the masked burglar, but there was nothing.

Putting on a kettle, he washed and shaved, dressed himself, made some tea and carrying this into his small study at the back, went upstairs and fetched the leather case. Sitting down at his disordered writing-table, he withdrew the contents and, laying them on the blotting pad, stared at them with wrinkled brows.

There was nothing to be learned from the key. It was of brass, and the maker's name had been carefully scraped off, apparently with a file. Anthony put it aside and turned his attention to the scrap of paper that had accompanied it, but although he puzzled his brains for nearly an hour, he could make nothing of the jumbled rows of figures and letters that covered it. At last, he drew a sheet of paper towards him and made a careful copy of the aged document—for aged it undoubtedly was.

The lines of figures and letters ran:

'M.O.C. V.2. P.101. L4. W.5. L.6. W.8. P.116.
L.2. W7-9. L20. W7. L.45. W6-9. L30. W.1. P.120.
L.10. W.3. L4. W5-6. P121. L19. W7-9.'

Having completed his copy, Anthony put the key and the original back in the wallet and slipped it into his hip pocket, and then, with a writing-pad and pencil before him, he tried every known form of deciphering the cryptogram. It was seven o'clock before he finally gave it up in despair and lifting the cover from his battered typewriter, began to bang out an account of his adventures of the previous night.

He read it through with pride when he had finished, and justly so, for it was a good 'story' and lacked none of those elements so dear to the heart of a news editor—and so rare. Putting it in his pocket, Anthony found that there was just time to boil himself an egg before setting off for the resplendent offices that housed the brains and pulsing heart of the *Courier*.

Mr. Downer, that greatly harassed and pessimistically-minded man, whose blue pencil had succeeded in breaking the hearts of more reporters than any other news editor in The Street, listened to what he had to say and read the closely-typed sheets without visible sign of interest. Reaching the end, he turned a weary and faded blue eye on Anthony—he had a habit of keeping the right permanently closed, and nobody could ever remember having seen both Mr. Downer's eyes open together.

"This is all right," he said dispassionately. "Wait a minute."

He picked up a pencil, scribbled an illegible scrawl across the top of the 'copy', slashed through half a dozen lines and, stretching out his hand, rang a bell.

"Take that to Mr. Short," he barked, throwing the manuscript to the boy who answered the summons, and Anthony saw his story whisked away to the sub-editor.

"I've told Short to 'splash' it—front page—banner headlines," remarked Mr. Downer, helping himself to a cigarette. "You'd better notify the police. There should be some further developments. 'Cover' the affair and let me know!" He drew a slip of paper towards him and scrawled on it signing his name. "Take this to the cashier for expenses. Goodbye!"

Without looking up, he began to search among the pile of papers littering his broad desk, and Anthony, who knew Mr. Downer rather well, and was therefore undismayed by the abrupt termination to the interview, picked up the slip he had thrown across to him, and left the office with a grin.

Strolling along the passage, he made his way to the reporters' room, and nodding to the solitary occupant—a red-headed man, who was industriously scribbling away at a desk in one corner—he picked up the telephone and within a few minutes was talking to an interested official at Scotland Yard. The conversation was lengthy, but apparently highly satisfactory, for Anthony's face still bore its cheerful smile when he finally hung up the receiver.

"You seem to have struck something," remarked the red-haired man looking up from his labours. "Couldn't help hearing what you said. Sounds interesting."

"It is," agreed Anthony. "What are you doing, Smith?"

Castleton Smith made a grimace of disgust.

"Writing up yesterday's dog show," he said lugubriously. "About as exciting as Tooting on a wet Sunday! All I know about dogs is that one end barks and the other doesn't!"

Anthony chuckled, and the other regarded him enviously.

"I wish I was doing your job," he remarked. "It's always been my ambition to run up against a real juicy murder."

"Every dog has his day," said Anthony sententiously and slammed the door to avoid the heavy directory that the exasperated Smith hurled at him.

He had reached the big vestibule of the offices before a thought suddenly struck him, and he retraced his steps towards a room on the second floor. Here were housed huge files containing back numbers of the *Courier* from the time when that enterprising journal first saw the light of day. After a ten minutes' search Anthony found what he wanted, and presently became engrossed in an account of the murder of Dr. Shard, the original owner of Whispering Beeches. Shorn of the embellishments supplied by the fertile imagination of the reporter who had 'covered' the case, the details were, briefly, as follows:

Four years ago, there had arrived, quietly and unheralded, from America, a middle-aged, retiring, rather shy man who had bought Whispering Beeches and settled down there with a small staff of servants. It soon leaked out that this unassuming personage was no other than Dr. Emanuel Shard, the famous cancer specialist, whose researches into the cause and cure of the dread disease were world-famous.

Immediately the house was besieged by reporters anxious to obtain an interview with the great man, but Dr. Shard refused to see any of them. He sent a message by his secretary and assistant—a man named Caryll—stating briefly that he was engaged upon experiments concerning a cure for cancer, that he had chosen the house for the sake of its quietness and didn't wish to be disturbed in his labours.

A year went by, during which Shard lived practically the life of a hermit, and his very existence became forgotten. And then one morning Duson, who combined the roles of butler, housekeeper, and general factotum, for Shard was eccentric and refused to have any women servants round him, found his master lying dead in his big laboratory at the back of his house, a knife buried to the hilt between his shoulder blades.

Recovering from his first horror at the discovery, Duson went to wake Caryll, but the secretary's bed had not been slept in, and he was nowhere in the house. The police were called in and a description of the missing man was circulated throughout the country, but without result. He had apparently vanished into thin air. Whether he had been the murderer or not was a matter for conjecture, for there was no clue to show the motive for the crime. Nothing had been stolen and no one had heard any quarrel between Shard and his assistant—in fact, the evidence showed that they were on the very best of terms.

The sensational crime had faded into the background, and finally became relegated to the limbo of forgotten things—one of those unsolved mysteries, remembered vaguely by the public, and worked on patiently by certain men who sit in a grim building overlooking the Thames Embankment. Such was the pith of the case, and when he had finished reading the various reports, Anthony Gale rose to his feet and left the offices of the *Courier* with a feeling of disappointment.

What it was he had expected to find he couldn't have said, but it had certainly occurred to him that this three-years-old crime might have had some bearing on the recent events in which he had become involved, and possibly thrown a light on the meaning of the cryptogram and the key.

The thought of the key turned his steps westwards. The unknown person or persons who killed Savini were obviously anxious to get it, and it would be just as well if it were placed beyond their reach. Anthony had an account at the Union and Southern Bank—so microscopic these days as to be barely noticeable, but still an account—and calling in he put the flat

37

leather case and its contents into an envelope, sealed it, and handed it over to be given up only on his personal application.

He experienced a sense of relief when he had done this, for the possession of that wallet, he was convinced, was a source of danger. His lack of sleep on the previous night was beginning to have its effect. He felt terribly tired and weary, and he was debating in his mind the advisability of returning to his cottage for a rest, when he became aware of a car that was moving slowly along in his wake.

There was nothing particularly extraordinary in this, except that Anthony was certain that he had seen it before that morning. It was a two-seater coupé, painted a dull green, and carried on the long radiator a peculiar-shaped mascot—a tiny silver model of the statue of Liberty. He remembered having seen it outside the *Courier* offices as he had come out, and again when he had left the bank. Someone was trailing him!

He stepped on the edge of the pavement and waited for the car to draw level, hoping to get a glimpse of the occupant as it went by. But in this he failed, for evidently becoming aware of his interest, the driver suddenly pressed on the accelerator, and the car shot forward, flashing past him and disappearing round the next turning without his being able to get more than a blurred impression of the muffled figure crouching behind the steering wheel. But still he had learned something. His movements were being carefully watched, and he had little doubt as to the reason. His foresight in lodging the key at his bank was justified.

On his way to the station to catch his train home he called into Scotland Yard but the man he wanted to see was out and not expected in until the following morning. Anthony scribbled a message for him and left, looking sharply about him as he emerged from under the big arch on to the Embankment. But though there was a stream of traffic passing in both directions, he could see no sign of the green coupé. The unknown trailer had apparently taken fright and given up the chase.

Anthony caught his train by the fraction of a minute, and so tired was he that he fell asleep and almost passed his station. It was with a feeling of intense satisfaction that he presently came to the gate of his cottage and paused, fumbling in his pocket for his latchkey. He had just taken out the bunch when he heard the whirr of wheels behind him and, turning, saw the green car flash by and go speeding up the road!

He smiled grimly as he walked up the little pathway to the front door. These people, whoever they were, did not mean to let him out of their sight, even though they must know that the thing they sought was no longer in his possession. Or didn't they know? Perhaps they hadn't connected his visit to the bank with the leather pouch and its mysterious contents.

Anthony inserted his key in the lock, opened the door and, nearly reeling with weariness, entered the small lobby beyond. The next moment he was wide awake and staring with horror at the scene before him. The hall was in a state of the utmost disorder. A chair was overturned, and the rugs lay crumpled up in a chaotic heap. But it was neither of these things that caused Anthony to rub his eyes and look again, wondering if he were dreaming. It was the man who sprawled in the middle of this confusion, for he was a complete stranger and he was dead!

CHAPTER 5

The Hooded Man

The light had gone from the sky, and the streetlamps were beginning to assert their dim brilliance, when a man descended from a big limousine car outside Lambeth North tube station, spoke a word to the neatly-uniformed chauffeur, and strode rapidly away towards Westminster. Passing the wide opening leading up to Waterloo, he dived down a narrow side turning, quickly traversed the dingy street, and swung round into another even meaner and dirtier than the first.

Halfway along this cul-de-sac—a high brick wall barred all exit from the other end—the man paused, and, glancing swiftly about him, took a key from the pocket of his heavy coat and approaching a grimy blistered door, unlocked it and entered. His feet thudded hollowly on the bare boards of the narrow, evil-smelling passage beyond, as, after closing the outer door, he made his way through to the back and unlocked a second door.

He stood looking out of this for a moment into the semi-darkness of a rubbish-littered wharf and listened to the faint lapping of water as the river brushed softly against the supporting piles, then, closing the door, but leaving it unlocked, he went back to the passage, and slowly mounted a flight of creaking, rickety stairs to the first floor.

Entering a room on the right of the landing, he felt for and clicked down the electric light switch, flooding the place with a soft light, and, crossing over to a wall cupboard, took out something which he proceeded to adjust carefully about his face. It was a hood of black silk, and into the eyepieces had been let squares of fine gauze which enabled the wearer to see without even his eyes being visible.

The room was sparsely furnished, a table and three chairs being all that it contained besides the cupboard, which hung near the bare mantelpiece. The windows were covered with shields of some tightly-stretched black material so carefully fitted that not a vestige of light could creep past.

The masked man shut the door and locked it, and then, seating himself at the table, drew some papers from his pocket and began to read. To judge from the appearance of his hands, he must have been well past middle age, for they were wrinkled and claw-like, the pallid, ivory-coloured skin stretched taut over the bony knuckles.

For some time, he sat motionless, perusing the pile of documents in front of him, and then of a sudden as a sound reached his ears from below, he gathered them up and returned them to his pocket.

There came the noise of a stumbling step on the stairs, and then, after a short pause, three taps on the door. The man in the mask rose silently from the table and went over, listening with his ear close to the panels.

"Who is that?" he asked in a low voice.

"Selton," was the hoarse reply, and apparently satisfied the unknown unlocked and opened the door.

A man entered hurriedly, blinking in the light, and the door was closed and re-locked behind him. The newcomer was short and dressed in a shabby suit of what had once been blue serge, but was now of a neutral colour, stained and shapeless. His face was long and unshaven and from his left cheek to the point of his chin ran the diagonal scar of an old knife wound. It twisted the corner of his mouth, giving him a perpetual sardonic leer.

"Why didn't you come in more quietly?" snapped the masked man, returning to his seat at the table. "Do you want to advertise our presence to the whole neighbourhood?"

"I can't see in the dark," snarled the other, flinging himself down in a chair and pulling out a paper packet of cheap cigarettes. "And them stairs are narrow."

His companion regarded him critically.

"You're drunk," he said coldly. "And when you're drunk, you're a fool, Selton."

"Maybe I am," growled Selton. "Maybe I'm going to be drunker." He lit his cigarette with a shaking hand. "Lacy's dead!" he burst out suddenly.

The masked man gave a slight start.

"Dead!" he echoed. "How did that happen?"

"They cut his throat," said Selton and his hoarse voice trembled. "That nosey reporter caught him last night while he was trying to find the key. Lacy waited until he went out this morning and returned to the cottage for another look. I waited outside to keep watch in case this fellow Gale, or whatever his name is, came back unexpected. After two hours, and Lacy hadn't come out, I wondered what was up, and went to look for him."

He paused and passed a shaking hand across his forehead which was dewed with beads of perspiration.

"I found him all right—in the 'all stone dead!" He shivered.

"Did they get the key?" asked the masked man, leaning forward.

"How the blazes do I know what they got?" cried Selton roughly. "They got Lacy and that's enough for me!" He brought his clenched fist down on the table with a bang. "I'm through! I'm not taking any more risks, not if there was a 'undred million in it."

"You're rattled," said the other contemptuously.

"Perhaps I am," snarled Selton. "And so would you be, if you'd seen what they done to Lacy. I'm goin' to quit and if you've got any sense, you'll do the same!"

"I shall do nothing of the kind," snapped the masked man. "There's a fortune waiting for someone in that house and I'm going to get it!" He drummed on the table with the tips of his repellent-looking fingers. "I wonder if they found the key?" he murmured thoughtfully.

"I don't care whether they did or not," grunted Selton truculently. "If you hadn't made a mess of things last night and dropped it after you'd taken it from Savini we might 'ave got away with it. As it is, Lacy's dead and I'm finished. I ain't going to have nothing more to do with it!" He glared across the table with bloodshot eyes. "Give me some money and I'll go!"

"You'll do no such thing," growled the masked man. "Or if you do, you'll get no money from me."

"Oh, won't I?" Selton leapt to his feet and stood swaying unsteadily. "We'll see about that. You think I don't know who you are. You think all this mask business has taken me in. Well, it hasn't! I know you all right, you old devil!" He staggered forward and gripped the edge of the table, his face thrust close to the other's. "And if you don't pay me, I'll squeal. Do you hear—I'll squeal!"

The masked man remained motionless, his eyes glaring behind the gauzed slits.

"So, you'll squeal, will you?" he said softly. "Selton, you're a fool to threaten me!"

"And I'll tell you something else," screamed Selton, half-mad with rage and drink. "That girl—you thought she'd come with Savini, didn't you? Well, she hadn't. She followed Savini and I know just why—see! I saw her this afternoon talkin' to someone. Do you know who it was? It was—" He lowered his voice, and almost whispered a name.

"Are you sure?" There was a note of alarm in the masked man's voice, and hearing it, Selton chuckled. "Now who's rattled?" he taunted. "Yes, I'm sure, and I don't blame you for gettin' the wind up. You didn't suspect she was in with them,

43

did you?" he broke off, and held out his hand. "Come on," he continued harshly. "I want some money and I want it quick!"

"I haven't any with me," answered the other. "Come back here tomorrow at this time and I'll have some waiting for you!"

"I want it now," said Selton with drunken obstinacy. "I ain't coming here anymore. If you haven't got it on you, I'll come with you to get it!"

There was a moment's silence, and then:

"All right," said the hooded man shortly. "Wait a moment!"

He rose, took off the black silk hood, unlocked the door and held it open. "Come on!" he said, and Selton passed out reluctantly into the blackness of the landing. He heard a click behind him as the unknown switched off the light and cursed as his feet stumbled on the first stair.

It was the last sound he ever uttered, for at that moment there came a dull 'Plop—plop!' Two spears of flame stabbed the darkness, and, with a choking cry, Selton went sliding down the stairs to lie crumpled at the bottom, an inert mass!

CHAPTER 6

Enter Mr. Budd

The big-faced man who sat smoking a big cigar in Anthony Gale's little sitting room early on the morning following his discovery of the dead man in the hall, might, from his appearance, have been put down as a prosperous farmer or a retired shopkeeper—in fact, anything but what he was—for Superintendent Robert Budd, known to his friends and enemies alike by the sobriquet 'The Rosebud', was as far removed from the popular conception of a detective as a Ford from a Rolls-Royce.

He was large and fat and lethargic; slow of movement, and never walked when it was possible to ride and never rode when it was possible to remain still. A veritable mountain of a man whose bulk overflowed the chair on which he sat, so that it seemed doubtful if he would ever be able to extricate himself from its embrace. And yet his brain was alert and, in contrast to his body, moved swiftly, for there was not a cleverer detective in the whole of Scotland Yard than this bovine, red-faced man, who listened silently while Anthony poured out the story of the mysterious happenings that had suddenly come into his life.

"Very interestin'" murmured Mr. Budd, gazing thoughtfully with a fishy eye at his evenly-burning cigar, "very interestin' indeed. I wish I'd been in when you called at the Yard yesterday, but I got the day off and went to a flower show." Horticulture was the big man's hobby, and it was partly for this reason that he had earned his nickname. There was a story told with great relish by the Assistant Commissioner of how the superintendent had once spent four hours discussing the relative beauties of dog roses and orchids with Pritchard, the Dorking murderer, before he finally remembered that he had come to arrest the man and executed the warrant that reposed in his pocket,

"Yes, I wish I'd been in yesterday," he continued with a sigh, "but the flowers were lovely. They had a new tea-rose there—"

"I'm not interested in roses," broke in Anthony, cutting short his reminiscences. "Let's stick to the matter in hand!"

The Rosebud looked at him reproachfully.

"All right," he said wearily. "They told me all about the murder at Whispering Beeches. Sergeant Wiles went down directly after you phoned and had a look round, but he found nothing except the bloodstains on the floor. Most of the other rooms in the house were locked."

"I know that," said the reporter. "Wiles came over to see me afterwards and questioned me for an hour just after I'd found that poor fellow in the hall!" He nodded towards the door and shivered. Even now he remembered the horror of that moment.

"You mean Lacy," remarked Mr. Budd, expelling a cloud of smoke, and Anthony looked astonished.

"Was that his name?" he asked.

"That was his name," replied the superintendent. "We've got his record and compared the fingerprints. He was a pretty tough customer, too—been convicted three times for robbery with violence. I wonder what he was doing there?"

"I believe he was the same man who broke in on the night I found Savini's body," declared Anthony. "There was a big bruise on the side of his face showing the marks of knuckles, and I hit him pretty hard," he added with satisfaction.

"Maybe," agreed Mr. Budd, nodding his head ponderously. "You think he came back again after you'd gone, to have another look for that wallet?"

"Yes," said Anthony.

"I believe you're right," The superintendent nodded again. "But the question is who killed him and why?"

Anthony made a gesture of despair.

"Ask me another," he exclaimed. "Who killed Savini? Why are they so anxious to get hold of that key and the paper?"

"And why should they kill the man who was sent to look for it?" interrupted the big man softly. "Was he killed because he had failed, or was he killed because they thought he had succeeded, or was he killed—" He broke off abruptly. "I'd like to have a look at that key and the cryptogram,"

"I'll get it," said Anthony. "We can go up to my bankers now if you like."

The Rosebud shook his head.

"There's no need for all that hurry," he said. "Tomorrow'll do." He paused. "I was thinkin' of going along to have a look at Whispering Beeches," he went on. "I've got the keys of the place from Tallents, Shard's solicitors. They tell me that most of the furniture's still there, same as when the old man was killed. That was a peculiar case. I was in charge of it—not that that made it peculiar. It was peculiar because we never found Caryll. There's no doubt that he killed the old chap, though nobody knows why. It's funny that the same sort of thing should have happened there again, isn't it?"

"Remarkably amusing," said Anthony sarcastically. "I find it difficult to refrain from laughing!"

"They've put me in charge of this case, too," went on the superintendent, ignoring the interruption. "I asked them if they'd let me handle it and they did."

"Why were you so keen?" inquired the reporter, struck by something in his tone.

"Because I always expected something else to happen at that house," said Mr. Budd, pulling steadily at his cigar, his heavy lids half closed. "I've been expecting it for three years.

47

You know the name it's got? Sinister House—and that's what it is, sinister."

He crushed out the stub of his cigar and with an effort hoisted himself out of the chair.

"I'm going there now. I thought perhaps you'd like to come with me," he said, pulling down his crumpled waistcoat. "That's one of the reasons why I called here first."

"What do you expect to find?" asked Anthony curiously, and the big man shrugged his massive shoulders.

"Everythin' and nothin'," he answered vaguely. "What is it these other people expect to find? Cobwebs, dust?" He shook his head. "There's something in that house so valuable," he continued, "that a murder more or less doesn't count if it helps to get it. And it's been there for three years."

"Budd," said Anthony seriously, "I believe you know more about this business than you've said."

The superintendent's fat face creased into innumerable wrinkles.

"Or perhaps I've said more than I know," he retorted softly. "Come along, let's go!"

They walked down the garden path to where an ancient two-seater car was waiting, and Mr. Budd, with some difficulty, squeezed himself into the seat behind the wheel.

Anthony had known the stout superintendent when he had walked a beat as a uniformed inspector, and before the C.I.D. had recognized his extraordinary capabilities, and between himself and the elder man existed a friendship that was all the more sincere because they seldom met, except casually, and then sometimes not for months at a time.

Anthony had kept Mollie's connection with the affair to himself, though he had been tempted several times that morning to take The Rosebud into his confidence. But second thoughts had prevailed, and he had kept silent. He was infernally worried about the girl. On the previous afternoon he

48

had rung her up as she had suggested, only to be informed that the girl was out, and on each successive occasion—eight in all—had been given the same message. Either she did not wish to speak to him, or she had gone away—his last call had been at one o'clock in the morning—and neither solution was particularly conducive to an easy mind.

As they swung into the avenue and drew up outside the broken gate of Whispering Beeches, Anthony could have sworn that he saw the green coupé disappearing up the road and mentioned the fact to the superintendent. Budd smiled as he got laboriously down and entered the weed-grown drive.

"You've got green cars on the brain," was his comment. "I don't think you need worry about that coupé. I—if it was the same car, it's miles away by now."

Anthony glanced at him sharply. He had a sudden feeling that the superintendent had ended his sentence differently to the way he had at first intended, but Budd was staring at the house ahead, his face expressionless. Even in the bright sunlight of that autumn morning it looked forbidding—a dark, gloomy pile of age-old red brick and grimy lichen-covered stone—the trees that grew around it were whispering mournfully as they shed their leaves in rustling cascades.

The big man went up the broken steps to the porch, taking a heavy bunch of keys from his pocket as he did so, and, selecting one, inserted it in the lock. It turned easily without a sound, and Mr. Budd grunted.

"Recently oiled," he muttered, and pushed the massive door inwards.

Even as it started to swing there came a scream from the drive behind them, and, turning sharply, Anthony saw the figure of a girl running swiftly towards them.

"Come away!" she screamed breathlessly as she ran. "Come away from that door."

It was Mollie Trayne!

CHAPTER 7

Mr. Jeffrey Tallent

The Rosebud looked round, his hand still on the knob, and the door open some two or three inches.

"Come away!" panted the girl. "There is danger there—terrible danger!"

"What kind of danger?" asked Mr. Budd softly, and to Anthony's astonishment seemed not at all surprised at the sudden appearance of Mollie.

"I don't know," she breathed. "But it's death to anyone who opens that door."

"H'm!" The stout superintendent rubbed his chin. "Well, the door's got to be opened somehow."

He looked about him thoughtfully, and presently his eyes lighted on a long wooden prop, part of an ancient pergola, that lay amongst the rank grass.

"The very thing," he murmured, and went over to it.

Returning with the pole, he placed it on the steps, one end against the door.

"Keep out of the way," he said, and Anthony drew the girl to one side.

Mr. Budd crouched in the shelter of the steps and, grasping the end of the prop, pushed firmly. The door swung open wide and at the same instant from within the dark hall came a shattering explosion! A cloud of acrid smoke rolled out of the entrance, and Anthony heard the angry drone of a score of bullets as they whizzed down the drive.

"That's that!" remarked Mr. Budd calmly and waited.

But after the one deafening report all was quiet, and presently The Rosebud, who remained by far the coolest of the trio, struggled to his feet and began to mount the short flight of moss-grown steps.

"For heaven's sake, be careful!" whispered Anthony huskily. "There may still be danger. There must have been more than one person lurking in the hall, and—"

The big superintendent shook his head gently.

"I don't think there is any more danger," he said quietly, "and I shall be surprised if there is anyone inside the house at all."

He looked back at Mollie, who was clinging to Anthony's arm, her face white and strained and her whole body trembling. "I'm right, aren't I, Miss Trayne?" he asked.

To the reporter's surprise the girl nodded. She was incapable of speech, for she was still breathing heavily from her recent exertion, but the quick movement of her head was sufficient answer.

Mr. Budd disappeared through the doorway into the dark interior beyond, and Anthony was racking his brains in a further futile attempt to solve the problem of Mollie's connection with this ill-omened house and the tragedy that seemed to envelop it, when he and the girl followed and passed into the gloomy hall. He felt her shiver slightly as they crossed the threshold and guessed that she was recalling the last time they had stood together on that spot.

The Rosebud was standing by the foot of the big staircase, gazing thoughtfully down at a peculiar object that appeared to have been fixed to the banisters. As Anthony and the girl approached, he looked round and rubbed softly at his upper lip with a fat forefinger.

"Most ingenious," he murmured gently; "very clever indeed."

He lowered his eyes once more to the object that had inspired this token of admiration, and following the direction of his gaze, Anthony saw in the dim light that filtered through the open front door a double-barrelled shotgun, which had been lashed securely to the newel post, the muzzle pointing directly

51

towards the entrance. He saw also the fine wire that was attached to the trigger and which ran through a tiny eyelet in the floor to a staple in the jamb, and from thence to a small hook screwed into the woodwork of the lower part of the door itself.

"Very clever indeed," murmured the superintendent again. "You see," he pointed to the wire, "the act of opening the front door pulled this wire taut and fired the gun. The wire being left sufficiently slack so as not to act until the door was pushed wide. A really brilliant idea, for it would be next to impossible for anybody to enter in the ordinary course of events without being riddled with bullets."

Mollie surveyed the murder trap with horror-filled eyes.

"I—I was only just in time," she muttered huskily.

"You were," agreed Mr. Budd, looking deliberately and ponderously about him. "Owing to my—er—rather generous proportions, I should undoubtedly have offered a very excellent target."

"It was certainly lucky for us," said Anthony, and then, turning to the girl curiously: "But what were you doing here at all? How did you know about this gun arrangement?"

"The intuition of women is notorious," remarked The Rosebud sententiously, before the girl had time to reply, "and cannot be accounted for in any practical way. It is sufficient that Miss Trayne was the means of saving us from—to put it mildly—a very—er—unpleasant experience."

Anthony stared at him in amazement not unmixed with a certain amount of annoyance. What was Budd getting at? As plainly as if he had put it in so many words, he was telling the girl not to answer his—Anthony's—question. Another thing that puzzled the reporter even more —the superintendent had twice addressed her by name, and so far as Anthony knew he had never seen her before in his life! It was all very puzzling and he began to feel that he had been swamped in a sea of mystery that had neither beginning nor end, and the very people from whom he might—with reason—expect candour and openness only made matters worse.

He opened his mouth to remonstrate on this state of affairs, but very wisely thought better of it, and remained silent. Later he would, perhaps, have an opportunity of questioning Mollie by herself, and learning something of the reason why she was so inextricably mixed up with the whole mysterious business.

Mr. Budd was engaged in peering up into the shadows of the staircase and was apparently oblivious of the thoughts to which his peculiarities had given rise in his friend's brain, for presently he turned with a genial smile and suggested that they might like to accompany him on a tour of the house.

"Not that I expect to find anything in particular," he remarked shrugging his broad shoulders. "But curiosity always was a weakness of mine, and I'm curious to know several things."

He paused for a moment, running his hand lightly up and down the flat oak rail of the banisters.

"For instance, I'm curious to know why there is so little dust on this staircase and such a lot everywhere else, and I'm curious to know why the hinges of that front door have been recently oiled, and why a man was murdered here two nights ago, and who it is who is in the habit of spending so much time in a house that has been shut up and empty for years and why—and above all, I'm curious to learn just why that gun was fixed to these stairs and for whom it was intended."

"It's easy enough to answer your last question," said Anthony.

Mr. Budd looked at him as though he were gazing over the tops of an invisible pair of glasses—a disconcerting trick he possessed when someone had made a remark that afforded him amusement.

"You think so?" he asked gently.

53

"Don't you?" demanded the young reporter. "Obviously it was intended for us. These people, whoever they are, must have got wind of the fact that you intended coming here to have a look round and planted that gun in order to put you out of the running."

"It sounds fine," said the big superintendent, but he shook his head all the same. "No, that gun wasn't put there for me— or you. It was put there—" He broke off and, bending slightly forward, listened intently.

The click of the gate came distinctly to Anthony's ears, followed by the sound of heavy steps crunching on the gravel. Somebody was coming up the drive!

Moving with extraordinary agility for one of his enormous bulk, Mr. Budd slipped past Anthony and the girl, and took up his stand in the shadow thrown by the open front door.

The footsteps approached rapidly, stopped for a moment at the foot of the steps, and then began to ascend slowly. Presently the figure of a man appeared silhouetted against the square of daylight—a short, rather wizened figure dressed in a tight-fitting black overcoat and carrying a neatly-furled umbrella. As it came into view, The Rosebud stepped forward and greeted the newcomer.

"Good morning, Mr. Tallent," he said pleasantly. "I am rather surprised to see you here, but as you see, I have lost no time in making use of the keys which you so kindly placed at my disposal."

The man in black gave a sharp, quick nod rather like an underfed bird pecking at a worm.

"I guessed it was you, superintendent," he said in a high reedy voice, "when I saw that the front door was open—in fact, I hoped to find you here."

As he came to a standstill on the top step, with the light full on him, Anthony was able to see him more clearly. He was an elderly man with a slither of grey side-whiskers and a long, hatchet-shaped face, which a large and aggressive nose rendered the more hawk-like. His eyes were almost entirely concealed beneath bushy, overhanging brows, and his mouth was a mere slit, with thin, bloodless and tightly-compressed lips that he appeared to be constantly drawing inwards. Altogether Mr. Tallent possessed anything but a prepossessing personality, Anthony concluded, and his feelings on this point seemed to be shared in no small degree by Mollie for he felt her fingers tighten on his arm and, looking down, surprised an expression that was akin to fear in her wide eyes.

"It is seldom that I find myself in this neighbourhood," the thin voice went on. "But as a matter of business brought me here this morning, and since I thought it was likely you might be somewhere on the—er—premises, I decided that I would call on the off chance, and accompany you during your survey of the house."

The lawyer cleared his throat.

"It is nearly two years now since I was here," he continued, "er—that is personally. My managing clerk, of course—er—pays a periodical visit of inspection and—"

Mr. Tallent suddenly became aware of the presence of Anthony and the girl and broke off abruptly, peering at them short-sightedly.

"This is a friend of mine," The Rosebud hastened to fill the rather sudden silence and introduced Anthony and Mollie.

The lawyer bowed stiffly.

"You were the young man who discovered the—er—tragedy here, were you not?" he asked and the reporter nodded. "A dreadful occurrence," said Mr. Tallent dismally shaking his head, "and absolutely ruinous to the value of the property. After the other affair, it was impossible to let it, but I was hoping that time would erase that unpleasant memory. Now, however—" He shook his head again and turned towards the superintendent.

"Am I too late?" he inquired. "Have you already completed your inspection of the place?"

"No, we have only just got here," answered The Rosebud.

"Then possibly I can be of assistance to you," said Mr. Tallent, "and also assure myself that the property is being kept in proper repair." He crossed the threshold and looked about the dusty hall. As his roving eyes encountered the murder-machine fixed to the stairs, he started perceptibly. "What—what is that?" he asked in a voice that was almost a croak.

The big superintendent regarded him with a fishy eye.

"That is what one might describe as a trap," he replied and proceeded to explain briefly the barrage that had greeted them when they had first arrived at the sinister house. Anthony noticed, however, that he omitted all reference to the part Mollie had played in that unpleasant episode.

Mr. Tallent's long lean face went white, or, to be more accurate, assumed a lighter shade of dusky grey as he listened in silence to Mr. Budd's graphic description, and at the end he emitted a sharp, hissing breath as though he had been holding it in check during the superintendent's recital.

"Good heavens!" he exclaimed. "What a dreadful thing! What a ghastly thing! Why, if I had arrived a few minutes earlier, I might easily have fallen a victim to this monstrous contraption."

The Rosebud nodded.

"Quite easily," he answered, and Anthony wondered whether he imagined the almost imperceptible stress he laid on the first word.

The lawyer stooped and examined the gun, touching it gingerly with his gloved hand. "I suppose there is no danger now?" he asked.

"Not the slightest," replied the big man. "It's as harmless as a boy's pop-gun."

Mr. Tallent slowly straightened up.

"Have you any idea what can be at the bottom of all these—er—extraordinary occurrences?" he inquired. "I should imagine there must be some—er—very good reason behind the recent events that have taken place in this house."

"I'm sure there is a very good reason," answered the superintendent heavily, "and if I knew what it was, I should feel a great deal happier than I do at the moment."

He consulted a large gold watch, which he took from his pocket with the slow deliberation common to men of his bulk.

"I should like to get my examination of the premises over as soon as possible," he continued. "I have a rather important engagement at lunchtime and—"

"Certainly, certainly," interposed the lawyer hastily. "I fear that I have unwittingly been the cause of delaying you, but, naturally, since I am—er—the trustee of the property, I take a considerable interest in the place. You will begin, of course, with this floor?"

To Anthony's surprise, Mr. Budd shook his large head.

"I should prefer to start by inspecting the basement," he murmured, "and also any cellars there may be."

"In that case I will remain here until you return," remarked the lawyer with a mirthless smile. "I am a martyr to rheumatism, and from what I can recall, the lower part of these premises is rather damp. You will find the way down through that door." He pointed with a black-gloved hand towards a door under the big staircase. "The key should be hanging on a nail beside it," he added.

Mr. Budd walked over to the door, found the key and unlocked it.

"Perhaps—er—the young lady would prefer to remain up here?" suggested the lawyer. "It is, no doubt, rather dirty and—"

"No—no, I'd like to go, too," broke in Mollie quickly, and Anthony decided that for some reason of her own she was terrified at the idea of being left alone with this gaunt man in black.

Mr. Tallent gave an almost imperceptible shrug of his thin shoulders.

"Very well, then," he remarked, and, taking a handkerchief from his breast-pocket, he spread it daintily on the lower stair and sat himself down. "You will find me waiting you when you return."

The Rosebud had already disappeared into the black depths beyond the narrow door, and, as Anthony and the girl gingerly made their way down the wooden stairway, they could hear him moving about below and caught a glimpse of light flashing along a broad, stone-flagged passage.

"Why are you afraid of that skinny old devil?" asked Anthony in a whisper, as they reached the bottom.

Mollie made no reply, and before he could repeat his question, the big superintendent joined them, holding in his hand an electric torch.

"Somebody has been here, and recently," he remarked in a low voice. "Look at those tracks in the dust."

He directed the light of the lamp on the floor, and Anthony saw a confused trail of footprints crossing and re-crossing the stone passage. Glancing aside, he saw something else and drew in his breath with a sharp hiss.

"What's that—over there by the wall?" he muttered huskily and, following the line of his pointing finger with the light, Mr. Budd uttered a quick exclamation and went over to the place.

Close up against the crumbling plaster was a dark patch, and it didn't need a second glance to assure him that it was dried blood!

CHAPTER 8

The Thing in the Cellar

Stooping, he looked at the sinister stain more closely, and then felt it with his finger.

"That wasn't made so very long ago, I'll swear," he remarked softly. "Now, the question is—how did it get here, and whose blood was it?"

Mollie, who was peering over his shoulder, suddenly gave a little cry and pointed to a spot a few yards farther along.

"There's another—there!" she said excitedly, and turning sharply The Rosebud flashed his light ahead.

The girl had spoken the truth. Not quite so close to the wall and smaller than the first, but plainly visible, was a second blood mark.

"This is getting interestin'," murmured Mr. Budd and moved over towards it.

"It looks to me as though somebody had passed along here who was wounded," commented Anthony, "though why they should have come here, heaven only knows."

"And the person himself—if he knew anything about it, which I'm inclined to doubt," said the superintendent cryptically, his eyes searching the stone flags that comprised the flooring. "Look, there are several more there!"

They went forward and found a regular trail of blood spots, that led them from the passage through a large, bare room that had evidently been the kitchen, to a heavy door set in the brick wall of a little washhouse beyond. In front of this door, they found the largest stain of all—a big irregular patch that had soaked into the dust and dirt that disuse and time had accumulated everywhere.

Mr. Budd paused and surveyed the door for a moment in silence. Then he raised his arm and attempted to turn the handle. But the door remained immovable.

"Humph!" he grunted disappointedly. "Locked! Now I wonder if the key's anywhere about."

They made a hasty search, but there was no sign of a key, and although the superintendent tried every key he carried with him, and even borrowed Anthony's bunch, none of them would fit.

"There's nothing for it but to break the door in," he remarked after he had exhausted them all, "for I don't intend to leave this place until I've seen what's on the other side."

Handing Anthony the electric torch, he placed his broad shoulder against the woodwork and pressed with all his force. At first nothing happened except a faint creak and then, suddenly, with a sharp crack, the screws supporting the lock were torn out and the door swung inwards. Mr. Budd went with it and, unable to regain his balance, was precipitated down a flight of four steps that lay beyond. He landed on the hard floor and uttered an exclamation that was more forceful than polite.

"Are you hurt?" inquired Anthony, anxiously, leaning through the open doorway of the cellar and flashing the torch into the gloom.

"Only my dignity," grunted Mr. Budd, scrambling to his feet. "Give me that light!"

He stretched out his hand and took the torch from Anthony's grasp, sweeping it round him.

The white beam, cutting through the darkness, revealed a fairly large apartment of white-washed brick, grimy and festooned with cobwebs. The low roof was raftered obviously with the beams that supported the floor above.

The place was littered with mouldering straw and pieces of rotting wood and smelt horribly earthy and damp and reminded the superintendent of a tomb. It was apparently the place in which the previous tenants of Whispering Beeches had stored their coal, for at the far end he made out dimly a dark heap that glinted in the ray from his torch.

There seemed nothing at all to reward him for his trouble in getting in and having taken a cursory glance round, he was in the act of turning to go back to Anthony and the girl, when something nearly hidden under a heap of straw attracted his attention. It looked like the corner of a leather case, of some description, and he went over to satisfy his curiosity, parting the straw to get a better view.

Anthony heard his suppressed cry and called to him sharply.

"Come here for a moment, will you?" said Mr. Budd and there was the faintest trace of a quiver in his voice. "No, don't bring Miss Trayne with you. Let her stay where she is."

Anthony gave Mollie's arm a reassuring squeeze and leaving her outside entered the cellar. The Rosebud was stooping down in one corner and as the young reporter stumbled to his side, he looked up quickly.

"See that?" he whispered, pointing to a figure that lay motionless amid a heap of straw. "That's where the blood came from!"

Anthony looked and went white and sick, for he was staring into the dead face of Louis Savini!

"Good heavens!" he muttered, "how horrible!"

Mr. Budd nodded and straightened his bulky form.

"The body was evidently brought here during the time you were unconscious"—he spoke rapidly in a low tone—"and I shall have something to say to Wiles for not finding it when he came and searched the house. Obviously, he never came down here at all, otherwise he couldn't have failed to see those bloodstains."

"But what was the object?" inquired Anthony. "Why did they go to the trouble of bringing the—the—"—he paused—"that—down here?"

"For the simple reason that if you had recovered consciousness and found the actual body in the room with you," answered the superintendent, "you would in all probability have called in the police then and there. Not finding it, they hoped that after reading that note you would decide to say nothing more about the affair. The last thing they wanted was any form of publicity attaching to this house." He looked down once more at the still and silent form of the dead man. "I'll call in at the nearest police station and send an ambulance to collect this poor chap's remains. In the meantime, I think we'd better keep this discovery to ourselves."

Anthony nodded dazedly. His brain was reeling with an effort to find some clear and convincing reason for the queer whirl of apparently disconnected incidents into which accident and his own curiosity had plunged him. Of only one thing was he certain, and that was that The Rosebud knew or guessed a great deal more about the whole matter than he said—and so also did Mollie. That to Anthony was the biggest mystery of the lot, and he determined at the first opportunity to have a long talk to the girl and try if possible to get her to confide in him.

As they left the cellar and emerged once more into the cold and dusty scullery, Mollie came forward and laid her hand on Mr. Budd's arm.

"What did you find?" she asked eagerly, her large blue eyes searching his face inquiringly.

"Quite a lot of dust," replied The Rosebud humorously, brushing himself down.

"But that wasn't all," Mollie insisted. "What did you call Tony for?"

"To kill a spider," explained the superintendent carefully. "I have an ingrained horror of spiders."

The girl gave an impatient exclamation.

"Why won't you tell me?" she demanded angrily. "You've found something in there—something important and I want to know what it was—"

"I found—" began Mr. Budd slowly and stopped.

From somewhere above them came the sound of a heavy thud—the closing of a door.

"What was that?" asked Anthony with a start, his nerves on edge.

"It sounded like the front door being slammed," answered the superintendent. "Perhaps old Tallent has got tired of waiting."

"Surely he'd have called down and said he was going," said Anthony and Mr. Budd shrugged his shoulders.

"There's no knowing what he'd do," he replied, "He's an eccentric old chap. Perhaps he only shut the door because he was feeling cold. However, we'll go up and see."

He led the way back through the kitchen and along the stone passage. Mollie lingered behind; her arm linked in Anthony's.

"Tell me what you found in that cellar," she whispered softly.

"Why are you so anxious to know?" he countered in the same tone.

"Because I'm curious," she answered.

"I'm curious about a lot of things concerning you," said Anthony, "but you won't tell me."

"Only because I can't," she said. "Honestly, I can't, Tony, or I would."

"Is that why you've been avoiding me lately?" he asked as they followed Mr. Budd up the stairs to the hall.

"Yes, partly," she replied candidly. "I knew you'd ask me hundreds of questions that I couldn't answer—and, besides, I've been very busy."

"What doing?" he demanded quickly.

"Oh, all sorts of things," she said evasively. "Now what was it you—"

The Rosebud's voice broke in upon her question, booming and echoing in the stillness of the vast hall.

"There's certainly nobody here," he remarked. "So, unless he's in some other part of the house he must have gone. Mr. Tallent!"

He raised his voice, calling loudly:

"Mr. Tallent! Mr. Tallent!"

But there was no reply. Only the hollow echoes of the name went rolling round the upper floors and were repeated faintly and mockingly.

"He's gone, or else he's taking a walk round the grounds," said Mr. Budd. "Well, in either case we can't waste any more time. We'll just have a quick look over the house and then go." He glanced at Anthony. "Which is the room where you found Savini?" he asked.

Anthony pointed to the door on the right of the hall.

"In there;" he replied, and the superintendent walked over to it, grasped the handle, and flung the door open.

"Come and show me—" he began, and then broke off sharply, standing rigid and motionless on the threshold of the room, his eyes staring, and his jaw dropped.

Anthony reached his side and looked in. The next moment he gave a cry in which horror and amazement were curiously mingled.

"Really, this is getting a trifle monotonous," remarked Mr. Budd wearily, and stepped into the room.

CHAPTER 9

The Disappearance of Anthony

Anthony Gale banged out the last word on his battered typewriter, collected the half-dozen sheets of neat typescript that strewed his writing table and, adding the one he had just finished working on, sat back in his chair and read through the result of his labours.

A satisfied smile played round his lips as he reached the end and clipped the sheets neatly together, for he had been typing an account of the latest developments in the Sinister House Mystery, as Mr. Downer had titled it, and for sheer sensationalism, Anthony concluded, it was calculated to please the heart of even that difficult and news-hardened man.

He folded the sheets, slipped them into an envelope, and laid them aside ready for the special messenger who was calling for them at nine o'clock to take them to the offices of the Courier for delivery into the tender keeping of the news-editor.

Stretching himself, Anthony rose and lighting a cigarette crossed over to the comfortable chair beside the glowing gas fire. The little clock that ticked cheerfully on the mantelpiece informed him that it was barely half-past seven so he had over an hour to idle away before the arrival of The Rosebud, who had promised to drop in and see him at eight-thirty.

Settling himself comfortably in the deep chair, Anthony allowed his mind to wander over the startling events of the day. After the discovery of the murdered lawyer on the exact spot where Savini had met his death, the stout superintendent had conducted a careful search of the entire house, but the result had proved disappointing.

There was little of interest, and nothing at all that shed any light upon the tragic happenings that had taken place within those grim and gloomy walls. Most of the rooms contained the original furniture, swathed in dustsheets that had been in use during Dr. Shard's residence, and the library and laboratory were practically intact, though everything was covered with a thick coating of dust.

Although they found no tangible clue to the meaning of the mystery that seemed to have its core in that weird and ill-omened mansion, there was plenty of evidence that others besides themselves had visited Whispering Beeches whilst it was unoccupied, for there were footmarks everywhere—footmarks of more than one person—and every drawer and cupboard in the place had been opened and ransacked. Even the books on the long shelves in the library had been moved from their resting places and tumbled in disorderly heaps on the floor, and in several places the rotting panelling had been torn bodily from the walls. Without the shadow of a doubt the house had been subjected to a rigorous search, but for what?

Anthony had put this very question to the stout Mr. Budd just before he had taken leave of that gentleman at the gate, after the arrival of the local inspector, but the superintendent had apparently grown suddenly deaf. That Budd had more than a vague idea as to the meaning of it all, Anthony felt certain, and he made up his mind to tackle him about his knowledge that evening.

His thoughts switched to Mollie. He had tried to persuade the girl to allow him to take her for a belated lunch, but she had pleaded a headache, and had even refused his company back to her flat. She had promised, however, to meet him for tea at Pelli's on the following afternoon, which had to some extent mitigated her rather abrupt departure.

Anthony had got one item of news which he thought would be of interest to Mr. Budd. The green car with the silver statue of Liberty had passed his cottage while he was in the act of putting his key in the lock, and this time he had managed to catch a glimpse of the occupants.

The driver he failed to recognize, but the slim figure seated by his side was unmistakable, for he had got a full view of her profile. What Mollie had been doing in the car which appeared to spend its time trailing him about had occupied Anthony's thoughts for most of the afternoon, but he had failed to reach any satisfactory conclusion, and had at last given it up in despair.

That the girl was a crook he steadfastly refused to believe, and yet she had been friendly with Savini; had obviously known about the presence of the murder-trap set for someone in the sinister house and was on intimate terms apparently with the owner of the green car.

It was true he knew very little about her. His first meeting with her six months previously had been the result of a request to pass the sugar in a popular teashop. From this small beginning had developed a friendship which had rapidly ripened into something more. A sort of vague understanding between them, which had been very pleasant until Savini had stepped in and spoiled it all.

Anthony sat on, letting his thoughts wander where they would, until a sharp rat-tat on the front door put an end to his reverie.

Mr. Budd stood on the step, buttoned up to the chin in a voluminous overcoat, his good-natured face one large expansive smile.

"I've been tremendously busy," he announced cheerfully, after he had divested himself of his enormous outer garment and carefully lowered his huge bulk into the largest of Anthony's chairs.

"That's a change," said the reporter. "I shall be interested to hear what you've been doing."

"You will, my boy," answered Mr. Budd, holding the drink Anthony had poured out for him in a chubby hand, and regarding it with a loving eye. "I've discovered something this afternoon which I have suspected for a long time but have never been lucky enough to prove."

"Well, what is it?" demanded Anthony impatiently.

The Rosebud looked at him over invisible glasses.

"I have discovered that Mr. Tallent was a crook," he said impressively.

He took a long drink and nodded.

"A crook!" he repeated. "And not only a crook, but a murderer!"

"Good heavens!" exclaimed the startled reporter. "You don't mean that he—Savini—" He broke off incoherently.

"No, no," replied The Rosebud. "If you mean did he kill Savini. I am referring to a gentleman of the name of Selton, who was discovered at six o'clock this evening in the hall of an empty house in Lambeth, shot in the back."

Anthony stared at him and passed a hand wearily across his forehead.

"I'm all mixed up," he said dazedly. "Who's Selton, anyway, and what's he got to do with it all?"

"I will explain," said Mr. Budd, emptying his glass and setting it down in the fender.

"It would be just as well," said Anthony sarcastically. "And while you're about it there are several other questions I'd like you to answer as well."

"'Ask and ye shall receive,'" quoted The Rosebud. "I'm in a communicative mood this evening."

"Well, that's something to be thankful for, anyway," said the reporter fervently. "Carry on—spill your end of it."

Mr. Budd reached over to the table for a cigarette and lighted it carefully.

"As I told you," he began, studying the glowing end intently, "we have for a long time had our suspicions regarding Tallent. Several odd rumours have reached our ears. Nothing very tangible, but sufficient to lead us to suppose that under the cloak of his legal business he was carrying on the illicit but profitable one of a 'fence.'"

"A what?" exclaimed the astonished Anthony.

"A receiver of stolen property," explained Mr. Budd, inhaling a deep breath of smoke.

"I know what you mean," said the reporter impatiently, "but a 'fence'—good lor'!"

"It does sound astonishing, doesn't it?" admitted the superintendent. "But it's a fact all the same. We have been practically sure of it for months, but we've never been able to collect a single atom of evidence against him—until today."
He paused and cleared his throat.

"Tallent's tragic death at Whispering Beeches gave us—or rather me—the opportunity of examining his private papers, and if there was a lack of evidence before there is certainly sufficient now. What a pity"—he shook his head sadly—"it is too late to act upon!"

"But what about this fellow Selton, or whatever his name is?" asked Anthony. "How does he come into it?"

"He doesn't come into it," replied The Rosebud with a sigh. "He's gone out of it. He went out of it, according to the divisional surgeon, thirty-six hours ago."

He took a long pull at his cigarette, slowly exhaled a cloud of smoke and continued:

"Among the various incriminating documents which we found in Tallent's private safe," said Mr. Budd, "was a book which set down clearly the many transactions in which he had been involved and also the names of the crooks with whom he had done business—an interestin' collection. There was mention, too, of an address in Lambeth at which apparently

Tallent was in the habit of meeting his criminal associates. I lost no time in visiting the place and found not only a considerable amount of further evidence against him, but at the foot of the stairs the dead body of a well-known little sneak-thief—Selton by name. He had been shot twice in the back and it was obviously a case of murder. The hand that struck down Tallent in that room at Whispering Beeches saved the hangman a job."

Anthony leant against the edge of the writing-table and thrust his hands into his pockets.

"What connection is there between all this and the other business?" he demanded. "What had Tallent got to do with that? You say he didn't kill Savini, so—"

Mr. Budd waved a fat hand protestingly.

"You go too fast," he objected. "The connection between the late lamented Mr. Tallent and the strange occurrences at Sinister House is slightly involved—so involved that I'm not even sure if my theory is the right one or not."

"What is your theory?" asked the reporter quickly.

The Rosebud carefully crushed out the stub of his cigarette in the ashtray.

"That would entail rather a long explanation," he began, "and I don't know whether I should be justified yet in—"

"Look here," broke in Anthony impatiently, "stop beating about the bush and answer me a plain question. Do you know what is at the bottom of these murders and the gun incident and all the rest of it?"

Mr. Budd considered once more, regarding his friend over the top of his invisible glasses.

"I have a very good idea," he replied after a slight pause. "Yes, I have a very good idea."

"Then for heaven's sake, let's hear it!" snapped the reporter.

"Unless I'm entirely wrong," said The Rosebud, "the whole thing hinges on the murder of Dr. Shard and the fact that he was engaged in trying to find a cure for cancer at the time of his death."

"What in the world has a cure for cancer got to do with it?" interrupted the reporter in amazement.

"Everything," said Mr. Budd decisively. "It is the motive behind the entire affair. It is the reason for Savini's murder. It was the reason for Dr. Shard's death originally, and it is the reason why the enterprising career of Mr. Tallent was cut off in its prime—a cure for cancer and a certain little key that is at the moment safely deposited at your bank."

"Do you think if you tried very hard," said Anthony wearily, "you could stop emulating the detective of fiction and tell me what you're driving at without talking in riddles?"

"I'm driving at this," replied The Rosebud; "Radium!"

"Eh!"

"Radium," repeated the superintendent.

"What the dickens do you mean by radium?" cried the exasperated Anthony.

"A rather rare substance obtained from pitch blend—" began Mr: Budd gently.

"I know what it is," shouted the reporter. "You needn't air your profound knowledge of chemistry,"

"There you are, you see," objected The Rosebud in an injured voice. "When I do speak plainly, you're not satisfied."

"Good heavens!" Anthony rubbed the back of his neck in despair. "Do you fondly imagine that you're speaking plainly when you keep on repeating the word like a—like a parrot?"

"If you didn't keep on interrupting me," said Mr. Budd, the chair creaking in protest as he crossed a massive leg, "I would try to make things clear to your dull intellect. That key which you picked up on the night Savini met his death—by the way I should like you to let me have it first thing in the morning—is the—"

He stopped abruptly as there came a loud, peremptory knock on the front door.

"That's my messenger from the *Courier* offices," said Anthony, glancing at the clock. "He's early—it's only ten to nine." He picked up the envelope from the writing-table. "I won't be a minute," he flung back over his shoulder and left the room.

The Rosebud heard him hurry along the tiny hall and open the front door, heard the faint murmur of a man's voice, then the slam of the door, followed by the sound of receding footsteps outside. Reaching out his hand he helped himself to a fresh cigarette and lighted it, flicking the used match neatly into Anthony's big ashtray.

A moment passed, but the reporter did not come back and, wondering what he was doing, Mr. Budd called to him. There was no reply. The superintendent called again louder, but nothing but silence answered him. With a sudden feeling of uneasiness, he hoisted himself out of the chair and went out into the darkened hall. The light from the open door of the room he had just left was sufficient to show him that the hall was empty.

Opening the front door, he looked out into the night. It was pitch dark, and a slight drizzle of rain had begun to fall, but there was no sign of Anthony. Mr. Budd walked down the little path and gazed up the deserted road right and left. The red taillight of a car was vanishing in the distance—a tiny spark that disappeared even as he watched it—but there was no other human life stirring.

Now thoroughly alarmed, The Rosebud retraced his steps and made a hurried search of the cottage. Except for himself, it was empty. Anthony had walked out of his study and vanished—as completely as though a giant hand had reached

72

out of the blackness of the night and snatched him from the world!

CHAPTER 10

The Man with the Ivory Hands

Anthony stirred uneasily, conscious of an unaccustomed restriction to his limbs and a dull throbbing in his head. Opening his eyes, he stared up at a low ceiling and tried unsuccessfully at first to force his still dazed brain into some semblance of normal action. Desperately he tried to recall what had happened.

He remembered leaving The Rosebud in the study at his cottage and going out into the hall to open the door to the messenger from the *Courier*, remembered facing a strange man on the step who had inquired his name in a low voice, and then something had sprayed in his face, and from that time until now had been a blank, or almost a blank. He had been dimly aware, as in a vague dream, of being caught as he fell forward in a pair of strong arms and carried somewhere, and later of the noise of an engine at close quarters. After that complete unconsciousness had descended upon him, broken only by one faint impression of rain falling on his face.

As the mists gradually rolled away from his senses, Anthony began to feel an intense curiosity concerning his immediate surroundings and, raising his aching head with difficulty, looked about him.

He was lying on a straw mattress in a long, narrow, low-roofed apartment that appeared to be some sort of cellar, or at any rate situated underground, for a musty, damp odour percolated to his nostrils and the bare brick walls glistened with drops of water. Near at hand was a large packing case, and on this stood an oil storm-lantern which supplied the sole means of illumination to this depressing chamber.

Opposite to where he lay, almost invisible in the shadows that cloaked that end of the room, was a heavy door. There was nothing else in the place, no other scrap of furniture beyond the mattress, and the packing case, if they could be dignified by such a name, and having seen all there was to see, Anthony turned his attention to the bonds that secured his wrists and ankles. A few seconds' experiment convinced him that they had been tied by an expert, for though he tried his utmost, the thin cords refused to yield a fraction of an inch.

He lay back again on the hard mattress and thought over his position. It was anything but a pleasant one, for he had no delusions as to who had been responsible for this audacious abduction or the reason he had been brought to this unsavoury place, wherever it was. Without a doubt it was the work of the people at whose hands Savini and Tallent had met their deaths. He wondered how long he had been unconscious, but there was no means of telling. It was impossible to see his wristwatch, for his hands had been tied behind his back.

It seemed to Anthony that an age passed before the faint sound of a shuffling footstep broke the silence. It came from the direction of the door and was followed almost at once by the rasping of a key in the lock. As Anthony stared across at it, the door began to open slowly, and there emerged out of the shadows the figure of a man. He was short and squat and dressed in a long black coat that reached almost to his heels. His face was entirely concealed beneath a black silk handkerchief that he wore around his head, and in which two slits had been cut for his eyes.

Moving in the circle of light cast by the lantern, with a curious shuffling gait as though his knees were perpetually bent, he stood regarding the prostrate figure of the young reporter in silence. Watching the sinister figure Anthony felt a little icy shiver trickle up his spine and the cause was neither the masked face, nor the evil glittering eyes that stared unblinkingly from the holes in the silk. It was the hands held half clenched in front of him. For they were long and talon-like, of the colour of old ivory, and so thin that the bones showed clearly. The hands of the man he had fought with in that empty room at Whispering Beeches on the night Louis Savini had been done to death!

"We meet again, Mr. Gale." The voice was gentle, almost musical, but with a sibilant hissing timbre that sounded indescribably menacing.

Anthony returned the other's steady gaze without flinching but remained silent.

"I regret that I have been forced to put you to this inconvenience," went on the masked man, loosely clasping his claw-like hands in front of him, "but unfortunately there was no other way. There is a slight service which it is in your power to render me, and which I am sure"—he laid a meaning stress on the last word—"you will not refuse."

"You seem to take a lot for granted."

Anthony raised his eyebrows slightly. The man in black inclined his head.

"Merely because," he said slowly, "I have a profound knowledge of human nature—and its weaknesses."

The words were ordinary and quietly spoken, almost whispered and yet they sent an involuntary shiver through Anthony as he heard them. There was a finality—an underlying threat in the tone of the voice that made his flesh creep. This shapeless figure in its long black coat, with those horrible ivory hands, radiated an almost palpable atmosphere of evil and something more—a relentless force of will that dominated. This creature would go to any lengths of devilry to attain his ends.

"What is it you want me to do?" asked Anthony after a slight pause, though he already guessed what the reply would be.

"A mere trifle," was the answer. "You have—or rather, you had—in your possession a leather wallet which you picked up in the hall at Whispering Beeches. If my information is correct, you have since deposited it with your bankers. All that I require you to do is write a letter to your bank manager, instructing him to hand that wallet over to the bearer of the note."

"Is that all?" inquired Anthony calmly.

"That is all," said the man in black.

"And after I've written this letter—what happens then?" continued the reporter in the same level voice.

"Yon will remain here for thirty-six hours," replied the other, "at the expiration of which time I will undertake to have you released."

"I see," said Anthony.

"You are prepared to do this?" There was a slight upward cadence in the tone and the only outward sign of excitement visible.

"No, I'll see you in hell first!" said Anthony without heat.

The man in black exhaled a sibilant breath and his eyes glittered through the slits in the silk handkerchief.

"I was hoping," he grated and failed to keep the fury out of his voice, "that you were going to be sensible."

"I think I am being very sensible," retorted Anthony.

"No doubt," sneered the other harshly, his hands so tightly clasped that the knuckles stood out white against the yellow skin. "However, I will believe that I shall be able to persuade you to do what I ask."

"There's nothing like being an optimist," said the reporter. "But if you think you are going to get hold of that wallet, you've made a big mistake. It'll remain where it is until I go and fetch it myself."

The masked man shook his head.

"I fear that you are labouring under a delusion," he hissed softly. "I assure you that I have several means at my command to enforce you doing what I desire."

He paused and leaned slightly forward.

"Several years ago," he continued speaking slowly and deliberately, so that every word received its full value, "I lived for some time in China—a marvellous country, Mr. Gale, and a marvellous race. They have evolved methods for persuading obstinate people to become—shall we say tractable?—that are extraordinarily ingenious and—er— painful."

Anthony compressed his lips. There was no mistaking the meaning that lay behind the cold ferocity of that emotionless voice.

"If you continue in your pig-headed refusal to write that necessary letter to your bank," went on the man in black, "I am afraid that I shall be compelled to initiate you into the more refined—er—methods invented by the Chinese." He gave a little cackling laugh. "Perhaps you may have heard of the wire jacket!"

The blood receded from Anthony's face, leaving it white and strained. He had heard of the wire jacket—that most diabolical of all the diabolical instruments invented for the torture of man by man,

"I see that you are well acquainted with the little—er—toy to which I have referred," chuckled the other. "Well, that makes it all the easier for you to understand what will inevitably be the result if you don't reconsider your decision."

The momentary feeling of cold fear left Anthony and was succeeded by a flaming wave of rage against this sneering, chuckling devil before him, that engulfed his senses in a red mist.

"You beastly mass of corrupt humanity!" he burst out hoarsely. "You can try all the damned tortures that you've picked up during your loathsome existence, but if you chop me into little pieces, I won't write that letter!"

The black-garbed figure drew in his breath with a sharp whistling sound and took a step forward. For a moment Anthony thought he was going to strike him, but with a supreme effort he mastered the rage that was consuming him and bending down, stared the reporter full in the face.

"We shall see," he said between his teeth and the words came like the hiss of a venomous snake. "I shall be interested to know whether, after the little demonstration I have in store for you, you will continue to remain in the same mind as you are at present."

Straightening up, he turned abruptly away and shuffled over to the door. Opening it he called softly into the blackness beyond. There was a long silence and then two other figures entered the cellar-like chamber. The first was a tall thin man enveloped in a soiled mackintosh and wearing a black handkerchief about his face similar to that worn by the man with the ivory hands. He was gripping the wrists of the second figure whose wide horror-filled eyes stared wildly about the dimly-lit chamber as she was dragged in roughly through the narrow doorway.

Anthony's heart almost stopped beating, and his throat went suddenly dry and hard as he recognized the white-faced girl. So, Mollie Trayne was to be the means by which he was to be forced to sign that letter.

CHAPTER 11

The Wire Mask

The short squat figure in the black coat gave a low malignant chuckle as he saw the expression of Anthony's face.

"Quite an unexpected development, eh, Mr. Gale?" he sneered. "And calculated rather to upset your heroic theories."

Anthony was silent, his eyes fixed on the slim figure of Mollie. She was in evening dress and her bare white arms and shoulders gleamed in the dim light of the lantern. A gag had been tied about her mouth, but the expression of her eyes as they met Anthony's spoke volumes. Amazement, horror and despair—a whole gamut of varying emotions changed swiftly in those blue depths but there was not a trace of fear. She was aware of her danger but still retained her nerve, and Anthony felt a little thrill of pride as he watched her calm, almost contemptuous bearing.

The masked man began speaking again softly and deliberately, obviously enjoying the situation.

"Before proceeding any further," he said, shuffling to the centre of the low room, and taking up a position so that he stood between Anthony and the girl, "I will give you a last chance to behave sensibly. Are you prepared to sign a letter on the lines that I have already suggested?"

Anthony hesitated. He guessed the reason for Mollie's presence, and the knowledge filled his soul with a cold dread. Anything was better than that she should be harmed. She evidently realized the struggle that was taking place within him, for he saw her give an almost imperceptible shake of her head. The action decided him. After all, if he could only gain time, something might happen. Budd would have discovered his absence, almost at once, and would immediately set the complicated machinery of Scotland Yard in motion. There was time enough to give in to this devil's demands at the last moment when every hope had gone.

"I will sign nothing," said Anthony shortly.

The other nodded his head slowly and made a gesture to the man who was standing by Mollie's side. Leaving the girl, he went out, carefully shutting the door behind him.

"It is a great pity," said the man in black when he had gone, "for the subsequent proceedings will be entirely your own fault. He paused and looked from Anthony to the girl and back again. "I think we were discussing the Chinese methods for breaking down the resistance of unruly prisoners," he continued quietly and his tone was almost conversational, "and if I remember rightly I mentioned the wire jacket. It is a cleverly constructed—er—little arrangement consisting of a cage of wire netting which is fastened about the upper part of the human body and screwed tight until the flesh protrudes in knobs through the mesh. The operator is armed with a sharp knife, and—no doubt your imagination can picture the result! I may add, however, that no one yet has succeeded in lasting out the full operation!"

He stopped, enjoying the look of horror and disgust that had crossed Anthony's face.

"I do not, however, intend to use that excellent arrangement in the present circumstances, so I have evolved, using the idea of the wire jacket as a working basis, a little instrument which I flatter myself to be particularly ingenious. Our friend has gone to fetch it and when he returns, I shall have great pleasure in giving you a practical demonstration."

In spite of Mollie's self-control, Anthony saw for the first time a glint of fear creep into her eyes and, for a second, she swayed slightly. She recovered herself almost at once, but the action had been sufficient to fill him with an almost overmastering rage against the cool, inhuman fiend who was speaking so easily, and callously of unnameable horrors.

81

The man in black must have seen the hot flush that mounted to the reporter's face, for he gave one of his little cackling laughs and leaned forward.

"Even now," he said, "it is not too late for you to avoid all—er—unpleasantness. Just a stroke of the pen at the foot of a letter that is already typed in preparation for your signature, and—you need worry no more."

"You're wasting your breath you nasty little maggot!" replied Anthony, though his heart was beating thunderously and there was a horrible sick sensation in the pit of his stomach.

The masked man shrugged his hunched shoulders.

"Then Miss Trayne has only you to thank for any—er—painful experience to which she may be subjected," he said harshly, and turned as the door opened and the other man entered.

He carried a large black box which he set down on the stone floor without speaking. The man with the ivory hands bent over it and raised the lid with a curious eagerness that Anthony found particularly revolting. Drawing out a strangely-shaped object of wire, he held it out in the light of the lantern and turned his head to face the reporter.

"I've no doubt," he said sneeringly, "that you are consumed with curiosity. Therefore, I will be as brief as possible. This mask which I have in my hand is my own improvement on the wire jacket. Its use I am about to show you."

He shuffled over to Mollie and with a quick movement slipped the thing over her head. It covered her face and neck with a network of small-meshed wire netting, and rather resembled the masks used for fencing, save that it fitted more closely.

"Keep still!" he rasped, as the terrified girl made a movement backwards. "It will not hurt you—yet."

He adjusted a screw at the back of the mask and then shuffled back to the box, from which stretched two thin wires up to the thing that enclosed the girl's face.

"Before going any further," said the man in black, with a chuckle, "I had better explain the principle on which my little invention works. In this box is a powerful battery, generating sufficient current to turn the wires of that mask round Miss Trayne's head white hot! It takes slightly over five minutes for them to reach the maximum temperature, but I can assure you that even at red heat the result is most—fascinating!"

A little strangled cry broke from Mollie's lips, and swaying she would have fallen if the other man hadn't caught her in his arms.

"I think she's fainted, guv'nor," he muttered in a deep voice, as he supported her slim, drooping form.

The man in black uttered a snarl of annoyance.

"Never mind," he rasped, "prop her up against the wall. She'll soon come to when I switch on the current—and she'll wish she hadn't!"

"You fiend!" burst out Anthony through lips that were white and bloodless. "You can't do it!"

"Can't I?" hissed the other and stretched out one of those horrible hands to the box. "I hate spoiling anything so beautiful, but you leave me no alternative."

His fingers groped inside the lid.

"Stop!" cried Anthony hoarsely, the perspiration standing out in little beads on his forehead. "Stop! I'll sign that letter!"

The masked man withdrew his hand and slowly straightened up.

"I thought you would," he said with a note of triumph in his voice. "Here!" He beckoned to the second man who was standing beside the limp figure of Mollie. "Leave the girl and come and untie his wrists."

He drew an automatic from the pocket of his coat and covered Anthony.

"A little precaution in case you should feel tempted to do anything rash," he sneered.

It took some time to loosen the cords about the reporter's wrists, for his struggles had tightened the knots, but it was done at last, and Anthony moved his cramped fingers about to restore the circulation.

"Here you are!" rasped the man in black and thrust a paper in front of him.

"Before I sign this," said Anthony, "I want to know what's going to happen to Miss Trayne?"

"She will be left here with you and released—after my messenger has returned safely from the bank," was the reply. "So be very careful that your signature is not likely to evoke comment, for in that case—" He left the sentence unfinished, but the threat was unmistakable.

With a shrug of his shoulders, Anthony took the pen that the second man held out to him.

"Alright," he said coolly, "you win."

Laying the paper on the stone floor, he leaned over the side of the mattress and signed his name.

"There you are!" he grunted and flung down the pen.

With an exultant laugh the man in black reached out a talon-like hand and picked up the letter.

"Bind his hands again," he ordered sharply, and in silence he was obeyed. "And the girl's ankles too, but take off the wire mask," he added, and again the order was carried out.

As soon as it was done the other man went out, leaving the door open.

"And now I will wish you a long farewell, Mr. Gale." The masked man folded the letter and put it in his pocket, shuffling towards the door. "I might as well tell you now," he went on, pausing on the threshold, "that I have no intention of coming

84

back to release you. I warned you once to keep out of my affairs—you foolishly ignored that warning. This time I shall take steps to make it impossible for you to—er—bother me again."

He went out, closing and locking the door, and Anthony heard his shuffling steps die away to silence. He looked over at Mollie. She was still seated, half-leaning against the wall, her head dropping forward on her breast. Anthony uttered a curse beneath his breath. He might have known that foul creature would never have let them go—had never had any intention of letting them go. He was racking his brains for a means of escape when a sudden sound made him raise his eyes quickly— a gurgling splashing sound that was rapidly growing louder! Over in the shadows a steady stream of water was falling— pouring out from an orifice in one of the walls! Even as he looked it increased in volume, throwing up a cloud of spray as it struck the stone floor of the cellar.

Anthony writhed and twisted in a vain endeavour to free himself from his bonds. Already the water was creeping in an uneven stream over the floor, and, at the rate it was entering, could scarcely take longer than half an hour at the most to engulf them! Helpless and panting from his futile exertions, Anthony lay back, watching the glittering cascade, and waited—for death!

CHAPTER 12

Night Shadows

Night had come and with it a fitful breeze that moaned through the beeches surrounding Sinister House, bending their skeleton heads so that they appeared to stoop and whisper to each other, and then draw angrily back as though annoyed at something they had heard.

Every now and again a pale moon gleamed momentarily from behind the wrack of leaden-hued clouds that were being driven mercilessly across the sky, and its white rays, touching for a second the twisted chimneys and gables of the gloomy pile, edged them with silver, so that from the roadway the place presented the appearance of a ghostly castle lifted bodily out of some ancient German legend.

Not that there was anyone about to see, for midnight had long since struck, and during those brief intervals when the moon peered down it shone blearily upon a sleeping world. And yet not altogether, for amid the tangle of rank grass and weeds and overgrown bushes that formed the grounds of Whispering Beeches something stirred—a vague shadow flitted out of the darkness and moved swiftly and noiselessly from tree to tree. Presently under the frowning wall of the house itself, it was joined by a second phantom shape that seemed to materialize suddenly from the surrounding gloom, and human whisperings floated up to blend with the voices of the trees.

A drizzle of fine rain had begun to fall, and after a moment's conversation the two black-garbed figures drew their coats closer about them and made their way stealthily towards the steps leading up to the front entrance. There was the click of metal against metal, and silently the big heavy door opened, the shadows melted into the yawning chasm of blackness beyond, and the door closed again, leaving a stillness more profound because of that momentary evidence of life, and broken only by the gentle patter of the rain and the intermittent sighing of the wind.

Inside the large, dusty hall, the two who had entered stood listening intently, and so dark was it that though they were but a few inches apart neither could see the other. Suddenly a dazzling beam of white light shone out and focused on the staircase as the shorter of the twain produced an electric torch, and the reflected rays showed clearly the ivory hand and claw-like fingers that encircled the smooth barrel.

"The only danger was that the police might have had the place guarded after I settled my little score with Tallent." The sibilant whisper sounded loud in that death-like silence, though the words were uttered almost inaudibly. "Still, I had a good look round earlier this evening, and again just before meeting you, and there was no sign of anybody."

"So did I," said the other and taller man. "There's nobody here—the place is deserted." He looked about him through the slits in the mask he wore and shivered. "All the same, I shall be glad when we have finished what we came for and get away. The house gives me the creeps."

His companion gave a low, cackling chuckle. "What are you afraid of?" he asked sneeringly. "Savini's ghost or—"

The tall man stopped him, clutching his arm quickly.

"For heaven's sake don't talk like that!" he said fearfully. "Let's get on with the job. What do we do first?"

"The library is our immediate objective," replied the owner of the torch. "After that we shall see."

He shuffled towards the staircase, flashing his light above him. The bare boards creaked in protest under their combined weight as they mounted swiftly, the shorter man leading the way and moving with a sureness that spoke of long familiarity with his surroundings.

Pausing at a door on the left of the first landing, he gripped the handle and pushed it open. The room beyond was large and oblong, and as he sent the rays of the torch dancing about, it revealed the dusty heaps of books piled everywhere in hopeless confusion—in stacks on the faded carpet; in scattered piles on the tables and chairs; thrust carelessly on the shelves with which the walls were lined. A strong musty smell of old paper and leather bindings greeted them as they entered and closed the door.

"It's not going to be easy to find what we want among all this rubbish!" snarled the man with the claw-like hands, his eyes behind the mask darting quickly about from side to side. "Did you bring the candles?"

The other nodded and produced them from his pocket.

"Light them and stick them on that table," was the order. The speaker was rapidly turning over a pile of books on a chair, examining the backs and putting them down again.

"What are you looking for?" asked the tall man, as he lighted three candles and stuck them to the large oak table in the centre of the room with melted wax. "You 'aven't told me yet."

"We're looking for a book—Morgan's Organic Chemistry, volume 2," snapped his companion shortly.

"A book—" began the other in astonishment.

"Yes," was the snarled reply. "Don't talk, come and help me to find it, or we shall be here all night."

He pocketed his torch and, stooping, began to look through the scattered volumes on the floor.

"You take the shelves," he grunted, "and let me know directly you find it."

For some time, they searched feverishly while the wind outside rattled at the window-sashes and whined mournfully round the angles of the house, mingling with the thud of each discarded book as it was hastily examined and thrown

88

impatiently down. A sudden draught flickered the candle flames and the tall man swung round with a startled exclamation.

"What's the matter? Have you found the book?" greeted the other, looking up quickly.

"No. Look—the door!" The reply came in a voice that trembled. "I thought you shut it!"

"So I did!"

The black-garbed, stooping figure twisted round. The door that he had closed stood open! Pulling a pistol from his pocket, he shuffled quickly across and peered out into the darkness of the landing, listening intently. There was no sound, only the patter of the rain on a window as the wind sprayed the drops against the glass.

"Must have been the wind," he muttered, coming back into the room. "The place is confoundedly draughty."

He shut the door again, and once more they began their search, though every now and again the tall man shot a nervous glance over his shoulder at the closed door.

Nearly an hour dragged slowly by, and then suddenly, with a cry of exultation, the short, squat figure straightened up, a large, green-covered volume clutched in one skinny hand.

"Got it!" he muttered, and limped hurriedly over to the table, his companion at his elbow.

Laying the book down he took from an inside pocket the worn leather wallet that Anthony had found in the hall, and with trembling fingers extracted the sheet of paper and the key. "Get your notebook and write down what I tell you," he ordered harshly, and the other, breathing quickly in his excitement, produced a pocket notepad.

With the sheet of jumbled letters and figures before him, the man with the ivory hands began to turn the pages of the book rapidly. At page 101 he stopped. The fifth word in the fourth line was marked with a pencil dot.

"Put down 'seventh'," he grunted, and his long lean forefinger moved to another pencilled word—the eighth in the sixth line. "Brick," he read out and the tall man added it to the word he had already scribbled. The other turned several pages and stopped again at 116. In the second line two words—the seventh and the ninth—bore the tiny mark against them, and 'left' and 'staple' were put down beside the others.

Comparing the letters and figures on the sheet with the figures and words in the book, the sinister figure crouching over the table spelt out the message, and at last, with an exclamation of triumph, he closed the heavy volume and flung it into a corner.

"At last!" he cried, tearing the notebook eagerly from the hands of the tall man and swiftly scanning the lines of pencilled writing, "At last! 'Seventh brick, left staple under bench, laboratory'," He chuckled hoarsely. "Come quickly, let us go and collect the fortune that awaits us behind that seventh brick."

Clutching the key in a claw-like hand, he shuffled to the door, a grotesque, evil figure in that fitful light.

"Bring a candle with you," he flung back over his shoulder as he hurried out on to the landing, and the other obeyed, never noticing in his excitement that he had jarred the table as he did so and as a result one of the candles had become dislodged and rolled on to the floor. It remained burning bluely as he followed his companion down the staircase to the hall below.

Turning sharply, the short, squat figure led the way to a door set in the wall immediately behind the stairs. Taking a key from his pocket, he unlocked it, and they entered a large, lofty room, the brick walls of which were covered with discoloured diagrams, grime-stained and festooned with cobwebs. The light of the candle which the tall man held was reflected from the collection of glass retorts, beakers, test-tubes, and an assortment of weird-looking instruments which loaded a plain deal table in the centre. One wall was covered with shelves on which stood countless bottles of every shape and size, and over all lay that eternal film of grey dust which seemed to enshroud the whole house like a winding sheet.

"This way. Bring the light over here," hissed the man with the ivory hands, going over to a long bench that ran underneath the window.

The tall man obeyed and, stooping, held the candle while the squat figure of the other crawled among the litter and dirt beneath the bench and searched along the wall. He found the staple quickly enough, and counting the seventh brick to the left, examined it carefully. In one corner protruded a rusty nail that had been driven in almost to the head and, grasping this in his repulsive-looking fingers, he tugged at it fiercely. It required all his strength to move the brick, for time had almost welded it to the others, but presently he felt it loosen, and a few seconds later had succeeded in pulling it bodily from the wall.

"Bring the light nearer—nearer to the hole," he said breathlessly, and when the other did so, he saw in the orifice that the dislodged brick had revealed a rusty square of metal in the centre of which was a tiny keyhole.

Panting with excitement and the exertions which his uncomfortable position entailed, he inserted the key. At first, it refused to turn either way, for the mechanism of the lock had rusted with long disuse, but putting forth all his strength, he eventually felt it grate round. A sharp jerk of the wrist and the metal plate swung open sideways on a hinge. Feeling about eagerly in the box-like cavity beyond, he brought to light a small object that weighed heavily as he held it between his fingers. It was a little leaden casket and, scrambling to his feet, he set it on the bench and burst into a shrill cackle of delight.

"Behold," he cried, rubbing his long, skinny hands together in ecstasy, "a fortune worth £200,000!"

The tall man eyed the casket doubtfully.

"It doesn't seem possible—" he began, but the other cut him short.

"But it is possible—it is a fact!" he exclaimed shrilly. "That casket contains the most precious substance in the world— radium!" He picked up the little leaden box and dropped it into his pocket. "Put back that brick!" he ordered harshly, "and let us get away from here!"

The tall man set the candle on the bench and stooped to obey. As he did so one of the claw-like, yellow hands flashed like lightning inside the coat, a knife glittered for a moment in the candlelight and the next was buried to the hilt between the other's shoulder-blades.

With one choking groan the body sagged forward, gave one convulsive shudder, and lay motionless.

The murderer looked down at it unemotionally except for the eyes, which shone evilly through the slits in the mask.

"You fool!" he muttered contemptuously. "Did you imagine that I should ever share with you? You've served your purpose and I have got my just reward."

"Not yet!" said a gentle voice from the doorway. "But it won't be long delayed, Shard—it won't be long delayed!"

The man in black swung round with a stifled cry and stared—into the smiling face of Mr. Robert Budd.

CHAPTER 13

A Remarkably Dangerous Man

The big superintendent advanced slowly, a long-barrelled Browning covering the cowering figure in black.

"I want you," he said in the same soft, almost apologetic tone, and when he spoke like that Mr. Budd was most dangerous. "Put up your hands—quick—right up to the beautiful sky!"

With a little snarling, animal-like noise, the other raised his long arms above his head.

"That's better!" The Rosebud nodded his satisfaction.

Keeping his eyes fixed on the man in front of him, he called to someone outside the door.

"Come and run over him and see what he's got in his pockets, will you?"

A figure appeared on the threshold, and as it came into the circle of light cast by the candle, the man in black gave a violent start, for he recognized Anthony Gale and behind him the white face of Mollie Trayne.

"Didn't expect to see me again, did you?" remarked the reporter pleasantly. "Thought I was drowned in that deathtrap of yours by the river. Well, I wasn't!"

"Damn you!" croaked the man called Shard, his voice choking with the fury that consumed him. "How did you get away? I suppose it was that interfering policeman!" He glared malignantly at Mr. Budd.

"No, it wasn't me," said The Rosebud, shaking his head. "If there's one thing I hate more than the criminal classes it's taking credit for something I don't deserve. It was a gentleman named Castleton Smith who spoilt your pretty little plan."

"That's right!" broke in a deep voice from the doorway, and Shard's eyes turned to a fourth figure, a freckled-faced young man who was lounging nonchalantly against the doorpost, smiling cheerfully. "Alone I did it! I arrived at Anthony's place just in time to see him whisked off in a motor car, having very generously offered to become a special messenger for that occasion only. The whole thing looked so fishy to me that I hung on the back, and when you arrived at that old house by the river, you were carrying an uninvited passenger.

"I didn't know how many of you there might be, so I decided not to butt in all on my lonesome but went and informed the local police. We were only just in time though. The water was up to Anthony's chin when we found him. I'm afraid we spoilt the party and soured your whole life, old thing." He tilted his hat further back on his head and grinned.

The man in black muttered something that was unintelligible, and Anthony felt his body trembling with the rage that possessed him as he swiftly ran through his pockets. He unearthed the automatic and the leaden casket and, slipping the former into his own pocket, looked up at the stolid Mr. Budd.

"That's all," he said. "What shall I do with this?" He held out the box.

"Keep it for the moment," said The Rosebud, "and take off that handkerchief that he's wearing. I should like to look upon his beauty unadorned."

With a swift jerk, the reporter pulled down the silk mask, revealing a long, deeply-lined yellow face distorted with such a diabolical expression of rage that it was scarcely human. The narrow slits of eyes peered out from the taut flesh malevolently, fixing themselves on the stout detective with a look that was evil incarnate.

"H'm, I'm not surprised you wore a mask," grunted Mr. Budd, and then sternly changing his tone: "Your name is John Shard, and I arrest you for the murder of your brother, Dr. Emanuel Shard, the murder of Louis Savini, the murder of

Jeffrey Tallent and that poor fellow over there." He jerked his head towards the still form lying motionless in the shadow of the bench. "There are several other charges, including the death of a gentleman named Caryll, but these will do to be going on with." There was a jingle of steel as he withdrew from his pocket a pair of handcuffs and held them out to Anthony. "Slip these on his wrists—" he began and was interrupted by a cry from Mollie.

"Tony—look!" she exclaimed fearfully from the doorway. "The house—it's on fire!"

Startled at the sudden sound of her voice, Mr. Budd involuntarily turned his head, and for the fraction of a second took his eyes off Shard. Almost instantly he remembered and jerked them back; but that momentary lapse of attention was enough for the murderer. With a tigerish spring, he leapt the intervening space between himself and the stout detective, sending Anthony flying with a powerful blow in his ribs, and gripping the pistol, wrenched it from Mr. Budd's grasp.

The whole action was so quickly carried out that the Scotland Yard man was taken completely by surprise, and before he could recover himself or make any move, he was looking into the muzzle of his own Browning held menacingly in the skinny, yellow hand of Shard.

With his thin lips curled in a wolfish snarl, the man in black backed slowly towards the door.

"Keep still, all of you!" he grated viciously. "I'll blow the first person who moves a finger, to hell!"

Still facing them, he crossed the threshold, and Mollie shrank away against the wall, feeling physically sick as he brushed by her. A weird red glow from above flickered spasmodically on his half-crouching figure as he reached the passage, so that he looked like some materialized demon from the underworld.

"You're all very clever," he snarled, "but I think the last laugh is with me. Neither do I intend to go empty-handed!" He shot a malevolent glance at the prostrate figure of Anthony. "I'll trouble you for that leaden box. Quick, throw it over to me! I've no time to waste!"

The words had scarcely left his lips when there came a thundering knock on the front door, and startled, Shard half-swung round in the direction of the sound. As he did so, moving with incredible speed for so large a man, Mr. Budd launched his huge form through the open doorway. There was a fusillade of shots as the murderer fired at him wildly, but luckily the bullets went wide, though Anthony felt the vicious hum of one as it flew past his head, and the next instant The Rosebud and his quarry were struggling in a confused heap on the floor.

The strength of that stunted shape, however, was enormous, for even as Anthony sprang forward to the detective's assistance, Shard succeeded in wrenching himself free and, leaping to his feet, went racing towards the staircase. But he had forgotten Castleton Smith. With a dexterous movement of his foot, that worthy young man tripped him up as he flew past, and with the added impetus of his flight Shard went headlong, falling with a crash on the parquet floor.

Before he could move, Anthony had flung himself on him, and when the panting Mr. Budd succeeded in staggering to his feet, he found Shard lying helpless and handcuffed, with the young reporter leaning against the wall wiping the perspiration from his streaming face and the hall filled with a confused babel of voices emanating from the half-dozen plain clothes men whom Mollie had admitted through the front door.

"We guessed there was something wrong when we saw the flames, sir," said a tall sergeant, going up to Mr. Budd. "The whole of the upper part of the house is blazing like a furnace and we were afraid you might have got trapped." He looked down at the handcuffed man. "Is this the fellow, sir?"

"That is the fellow," answered The Rosebud carefully. "Take him along sergeant, and keep a strong guard over him, for he is a remarkably dangerous man!"

*   *   *   *

In spite of the efforts of the hastily summoned fire-brigade, it was impossible to save Whispering Beeches from the devouring flames. The old house with its panelled walls and oak beams, burned like tinder, and when dawn broke greyly there was nothing left of the gloomy, ill-omened mansion except a heap of smouldering blackened ruins and part of the wall that reared its solitary bulk, a silent epitaph to that which was no more, against the rapidly lighting sky.

The stout Mr. Budd did not wait for the end, but accompanied his prisoner back to Cannon Row, which adjoins Scotland Yard, and in a bare and cheerless cell subjected him to a close examination.

It was a long time before Shard could be persuaded to break the sullen silence which he had maintained since his capture, but eventually, realizing that everything was hopeless, he did so, and the story that he told tore the last veil from the mystery surrounding Sinister House.

It was the following evening before The Rosebud found time to satisfy the curiosity of an impatient Anthony, and then in the cosy sitting room of Mollie Trayne's flat he unfolded the sequence of events which had led up to, and formed part of the strange drama that ended with the holocaust that destroyed its setting.

Everybody will remember the full-page article which appeared under the name of Anthony Gale in the *Courier*, and which caused the taciturn Mr. Downer to smile for the first and last time in his life. So, it is only necessary to touch on the salient points in the story that The Rosebud recounted as they sat round Mollie's cheerful fire and listened to the stout detective's laborious sentences.

"John Shard, as you already know, was Dr. Emanuel's brother, he began. "A careless nurse who dropped him when he was a year old was the cause of his physical deformity. Whether this also affected him mentally is impossible to say, but from an early age he developed criminal tendencies, and was always in trouble of one sort or another. Before he was twenty-four, he had served several short sentences for minor robberies in America, and in spite of his elder brother's efforts to reform him he went from bad to worse. Eventually, having made New York too hot to hold him, he disappeared, and his brother lost all trace of him."

The Rosebud paused, took a cigar from his pocket, looked at the girl for permission to smoke, and lit it carefully.

"According to his own account," he continued after two or three slow puffs, "he spent several years in China and then drifted to South Africa. Here he got mixed up with illicit diamond buying and was sentenced to five years in Pretoria Central, afterwards being transferred to the Breakwater. About the same time as Dr. Shard arrived in England, his brother succeeded in escaping from the Breakwater. Penniless and hunted—how he evaded capture is a mystery to me—he saw one day a short paragraph in a newspaper mentioning his brother's whereabouts and decided to seek him out and obtain help. By devious routes he worked his way to London, and almost the first person he met on his arrival was Louis Savini, an international crook whom he had known intimately in America. Savini was working at the time with Tallent, who 'fenced' the proceeds of the various robberies carried out by the gang they jointly controlled. Tallent had learnt that, for the purposes of his experiments, Dr. Shard had in his possession a quantity of radium, close on £200,000 worth, which had been loaned to him by the State College of Research in America, and for some time Tallent had been trying to devise a plan by which he and Savini could get this valuable substance into their own hands.

"Dr. Shard was a nervous man and careful inquiries had elicited the fact that not even his secretary, Caryll, knew where he kept his stock of the rare salt, the experiments for which it was used being carried out by the doctor alone behind locked doors. He had, however, taken the precaution of setting down in cipher form the place where it was hidden, and had told Caryll that the key was to be found in Morgan's Organic Chemistry, volume 2. The cipher itself he carried about with him in a leather wallet. He had suffered for a long time with his heart, and it was only if anything should happen to him that the secretary was instructed to return the radium to the College of Research where it belonged. These precautions seem, I'll admit, rather ridiculous, but you must take into account the fact that he was undoubtedly eccentric, that the radium was of great value and was, moreover, only loaned to him. To cut a long story short Tallent and Savini learned these facts—except the fact that Caryll knew the key to the cipher—by getting Selton, who was a member of their gang, a job as gardener at Whispering Beeches.

"When Savini found out that Shard was the doctor's brother he took him into their confidence and outlined a plan which he and Tallent had previously formed and were going to carry out on their own. It was simple in the extreme.

"Doctor Shard was in the habit of working far into the night and armed with a duplicate key to the laboratory and the back door—which of course Tallent, who let the property, had in his possession—Savini and Selton were to take him by surprise late one night and force him to reveal where the radium was kept. On the night when Dr. Shard was murdered the scheme was carried out, the only alteration being that they substituted John Shard for Selton, but Tallent and Savini had not reckoned on the fits of demoniacal rage that occasionally took possession of the hunchback, and this was their undoing.

"They found the doctor in his laboratory, and Savini, according to plan, waited in the hall while Shard went in to his brother. It was because they thought that Shard was less likely to give the alarm if he was suddenly confronted by his own brother that he had been chosen instead of Selton. Dr. Shard was so furious at the sight of his brother that he threatened all sorts of things if he didn't go immediately, and finally he aroused the other's temper to such a degree that John Shard stabbed him. His rage subsided directly he realized what he had done, but it was too late. His brother was already dead, and with him had died the secret of where the radium was hidden.

Shard called in Savini, and they held a hurried consultation. It was useless to try and extract information from a dead man, so they made a swift search of the laboratory, but without finding what they sought. Savini remembered the cipher, and in the doctor's pocket they found the leather wallet containing it and the small key. But without Caryll it was useless—he alone knew where the solution to that jumble was to be found.

"Shard and Savini had decided to give it up and get away while they were safe, when Caryll who had been out late, returned and caught them. Before he had time, however, to give the alarm, Shard knocked him senseless, and it was then he suggested that they should kidnap him and make him reveal the secret of the cipher message. They took him to an old house by the river at Wraysbury, which belonged to Tallent, and where Shard had been living—the same by the way where you and Miss Trayne nearly met your deaths, and here Shard tried by every evil means in his power to force Caryll to speak. What tortures the unfortunate man went through we can, knowing Shard, imagine, and at last he told the hunchback what he

100

wanted to know. But the strain he had undergone during the intervening period proved too much for him. He died and Shard buried the body in the garden.

"The position was now this—Savini and Tallent had the cipher and Shard had the key to it, for he had been alone when Caryll finally spoke, and neither was of use without the other. Knowing this Shard refused to part with his knowledge unless he received two-thirds of the proceeds instead of one-third, which had been originally agreed upon. The situation developed into a feud between Shard and Tallent, which lasted for nearly three years, while each was trying to get the information required from the other. At last Shard managed to lure Savini into Sinister House—killed him and secured the wallet which he afterwards lost during his fight with you."

Mr. Budd drew a long breath and leaned back to the imminent peril of Mollie's chair.

"The rest you know," he said.

"There's one thing still I don't understand," declared Anthony after a pause. "What part did Mollie play in all this?"

The Rosebud smiled and looked across at the girl with a wink.

"Shall I tell him?" he asked. "Or will you?"

"You tell him," answered Mollie quickly.

The superintendent cleared his throat.

"When the death of Shard became known in America," he said, "the State College of Research became anxious about their radium, and got in touch with the American police, who communicated with Scotland Yard. We did our best but had to cable eventually that we could find no trace of it. The president of the College, however, wasn't satisfied, and enlisted the aid of Pinkerton's, and—" The Rosebud stopped and chuckled—"and there you are!" he added.

A light suddenly dawned on Anthony's brain.

"You mean?" he almost shouted, rising to his feet.

"They sent over the best detective I have ever met," said Mr. Budd. "She ought to have all the credit, for it was she who found out that John Shard was in England and discovered his and Savini's connections with the case. It was while she was following Savini on the night of his murder that Shard chloroformed her. Luckily, he thought she was only a friend of Savini's. If he'd guessed the truth, I don't suppose she would be alive now."

"I spent most of my time following you about," put in Mollie smiling up into Anthony's amazed eyes.

"Then the green car was yours?" he stuttered dazedly.

"Yes, I brought it with me from New York. It's a wonderful machine."

"You're a wonderful girl," said The Rosebud admiringly.

"She is!" declared Anthony fervently; "and—"

"I think I'll go and have a look at that new florist's in Regent Street," remarked Mr. Budd softly, and discreetly withdrew.

THE END

MR. K.

CHAPTER 1

Wrong Number!

The most trivial decisions have a habit of leading to momentous events. If Peter Lake had not elected to walk home from George Arlington's on that hot summer night, the whole course of his life might have been changed. He would in all probability never have met Lola Marsh; remained ignorant of the existence of the elusive 'Mr. K.' and avoided the danger and unpleasantness surrounding the green fountain pen belonging to the unfortunate Harvey Slade.

But fate, which is another name for circumstance, willed it otherwise, and so, when he set off along the cool and deserted country lane which led to the village, he took the first step that was to lead him out of the commonplace routine of his daily life and plunge him into an uncharted sea of mystery, danger and sudden death!

He refused George Arlington's offer of a lift because he was a little worried and hoped that the mile and a quarter walk would produce something in the nature of a solution to the problem that was bothering him. It was a very prosaic problem and centred round a collection of unpaid bills that almost filled a small drawer of the desk in his shabby consulting room, but it was also a very vital problem, and had caused Peter to lose a considerable amount of sleep during the past few weeks.

He needed money urgently—at least three of his creditors were getting unpleasantly pressing—and Peter had not the remotest idea where the money could be obtained. He had sunk every penny of his small capital in the purchase of old Dr. Heppel's practice and had bitterly regretted it before he had been in occupation a month.

The chief source of income had been an eccentric old lady, who had nothing the matter with her at all, except old age, but

105

who liked to have a doctor in daily attendance on her and was willing to pay for this privilege. Her only complaint had carried her off a fortnight after Peter had moved into the little house on the fringe of the village, and the remainder of his patients were disgustingly healthy.

He had carried on, hoping for the best, and getting more and more into debt until now the crisis was almost at hand. Between now and Saturday—three days—it was absolutely essential that he should find a hundred and fifty pounds, and he hadn't the least idea where to find even a hundred and fifty pence. Nothing short of a miracle or an epidemic could save him from the resultant proceedings.

He lit a cigarette, thrust his hands into the pockets of his dinner-jacket, and frowned.

His last forlorn effort had failed.

It had taken a certain amount of moral courage to ask George Arlington for help, and although George had been very sympathetic, he had made it quite clear that he could do nothing, and sympathy wasn't going to stop Macklinbergs from issuing a writ. The prospect looked black—almost as black as the clouded sky. The association of ideas made him look up, and as he did so a jagged ribbon of blue flickered in the south. It was followed a few seconds later by the low mutter of thunder.

Peter turned up the collar of his jacket and broke into a run, but before he had gone a hundred yards the rain was coming down in torrents. There was no shelter. The lane was narrow, and ran between straggling hedges, enclosed by barbed wire, beyond which lay ploughed fields. He had reached a point where a secondary road bisected the lane, and had resigned himself to a soaking, when in the brilliant glare of the lightning he saw the very thing he wanted.

At the junction of the roads stood a public callbox. Peter made for it as fast as he could, jerked open the door, and stumbled into the interior with a sigh of thankfulness. The rain was falling with almost tropical violence, hissing and splashing round his tiny shelter; the lightning and thunder were almost incessant. However, it was dry enough inside the telephone box, and he could stay until the storm passed over. He took his handkerchief from his pocket, and wiped the wet from his hair and neck, wondering why he had not remembered this place before. He had passed it often enough.

Replacing the handkerchief, he took out a cigarette, and was in the act of feeling for his lighter when the bell behind him rang shrilly—a deafening racket in that confined space. Peter jumped violently and swung round, staring at the dimly seen instrument.

Who the deuce could be ringing up a public call-box? The bell ceased for a moment and then started again—an insistent and prolonged br-r-r—

More from curiosity than anything else, Peter lifted the receiver from its hook and put it to his ear.

"Hello!" he called, and almost instantly there came over the wire the faint, breathless, agitated voice of a girl.

"Jim! Jim! Is that you?" she said, and then before he could answer: "For heaven's sake come to Slade's at once!"

"I'm afraid—" began Peter, but the caller went on quickly without listening.

"I'm frightened—horribly frightened." The tone was frantic; the words jerky and disjointed; barely audible. "He's locked me in…there's something dreadful going on… 'Mr. K.'—" There was a rasping, scraping sound, the echo of a scream, and—silence.

For a second Peter stood still, the memory of that soft frightened voice ringing in his ears, and then he dropped the receiver back on its hook. There was no mistaking the meaning of that scraping sound—someone had cut the telephone wires while the girl had been speaking.

Peter frowned. She had mentioned Slade's. That must mean Harvey Slade, surely—the occupier of the big gaunt house on the left of the secondary road barely a hundred and fifty yards away. What was going on there? Something pretty bad, apparently. Peter could still hear that terror-laden voice with its urgent appeal. Well, rain or no rain, he wasn't going to leave a girl in that state without seeing what was happening.

He had evidently received a message intended for Jim, whoever he was—probably the exchange had plugged into the wrong number. He pulled open the door of the little kiosk and stepped out into the downpour. If anything, it had increased, and before he had gone a dozen yards he was soaked to the skin, with his hair hanging in straggling wisps over his forehead.

Locked her in, had they? His thoughts were grim as he splashed his way along the right-hand branch of the secondary road. Well, they'd damn well soon have to let her out again. Just the sort of thing he would expect from a man like old Slade—a thin, bald-headed old vulture, hated by everybody in the village, and Peter in particular. He was in sight of the house now—a low rambling building set well back among a cluster of trees—a dark repellent place with no light visible at any of the windows. A long drive ran up from the road, bordered on either side by high, dense hedges, each leaf a miniature cataract.

Peter entered the open gateway, and as he did so there came from somewhere ahead a muffled cry; a scream of sheer terror that pulled him up in his tracks and stirred the hair on his neck. There was death in that awful cry. It came again, but this time was drowned in the crash of thunder that split the heavens and shook the ground under his feet.

He took a step forward, and then, as the echoes of the thunderclap rumbled to silence, he heard another sound—the sound of someone running rapidly, desperately. He crouched back against the gatepost, his nerves tense, watching the dark

108

tunnel of the drive down which those flying steps were coming. They drew nearer and nearer, and now he could hear the panting breaths of the runner. And then the lightning glared fitfully, and in its bluish radiance he saw the figure of a big man coming towards him with surprising speed considering his bulk.

He straightened up as the man bore down upon him and shouted to him to stop. The reply he received was unexpected. He heard a muttered oath, and out of the darkness came a stab of flame, and the crack of an automatic. The bullet sped past Peter without danger, but he felt the wind of it unpleasantly close to his right ear.

Peter was not unreasonably annoyed, and as the shooter drew level with him, he stepped forward and lashed out with his right. He brought all the weight of his thirteen stone to bear on that blow, and it caught the runner on the side of the jaw. With a yelp of pain, he staggered and fell sprawling. Had it reached the point, as Peter intended it should, he would have stayed down, but as it was it only stunned him for a second, and as Peter stooped over him, he kicked out viciously with his feet. One of his heavy boots landed with a terrific impact on Peter's right knee and he collapsed.

In a second the other was up and, taking to his heels, disappeared through the gateway into the darkness and rain. Peter scrambled to his feet shakily and painfully. He was smothered in mud from head to foot, and his knee was hurting like the deuce. He tested his weight gingerly on his injured leg and found that it was not as bad as he thought. He was moving forward, when he trod on something that was hard and round. He thought that it was a stone at first, and then the lightning came again and looking down he saw something that glinted greenly on the gravel of the path.

Stooping he picked it up, and striking a match, saw that it was a fountainpen. The big man must have dropped it when he fell. Almost unconsciously, Peter slipped it into his jacket pocket, and from that moment went in danger of his life, for the green fountainpen carried in its train the shadow of death!

CHAPTER 2

'Mr. K.'

Peter made his way slowly up the drive, keeping a wary lookout for anyone else who might be lurking about. But he saw no one. The place was apparently deserted.

Presently he came underneath the dark bulk of the house and looked up. There was still no light to be seen anywhere, nor could he hear any sound save the swish of the falling rain on the leaves. He went up the steps to the front door and found rather to his surprise that it was half open, the hall beyond being in pitch darkness.

After a momentary hesitation he cautiously crossed the threshold and listened. But still no sound came to his straining ears. An unearthly hush seemed to brood like a living presence over the whole house.

He stood rather undecidedly just inside the doorway. There must be somebody about. From whom had come those horrible screams? And where was the girl whose voice he had heard over the telephone? It was certainly not she who had screamed; the tone had been deeper, that of a man. Of course, she had said something about being locked in.

He hesitated no longer, but moving forward into the darkness of the hall, fumbled along the wall in the hope of finding the electric light switches. After a moment or two he found them and pressing them down, flooded the place with a blaze of light.

The hall was beautifully furnished. The light, streaming down from silk-shaded pendants, was reflected in the polished furniture and showed up the warm colours of the rugs with which the parquet floor was strewn. Peter, who knew about such things, took a mental note of the pictures on the walls. A Marillo, one or two of Zhon's etchings—a Millais, Old Harvey

111

Slade, for all his reputed meanness, evidently liked to surround himself with good things.

With the lights on, Peter felt a little less uncomfortable. He was still a trifle apprehensive in this silent house; the atmosphere was oppressive, but the light gave the added assurance of sight. He was no longer groping in the dark against a horror that was invisible. Whatever might be lurking in wait for him there, it was a pleasant relief to know that he could see it coming.

Several rooms opened off the hall, but before approaching any of them, he called loudly:

"Anybody at home?"

His voice came back to him with a booming echo from the darkness of the big staircase, but nobody answered. He went over to the first door, pushed it open, switched on the lights, and peered in. It was the dining-room, evidently, and empty. Someone, however, had used it recently, for the centre table was still laid with the remains of a meal.

His frown deepened as he went to the second door. What the deuce was the matter with this house? There was something frightening about this unbroken silence. Surely there were servants in a big place like this, and where were they? Mechanically he glanced at his wristwatch. It was nearly half-past eleven. They couldn't still be out at this hour. And those screams—

He gave an involuntary shudder as he pushed open the second door and looked in. The lights here were on—he had not seen them before because the window gave on to the back of the house—and one glance told him that he need look no farther for an explanation of those terrible cries! It was here, in this lighted room, lying sprawled by the side of the big desk. A twisted figure, whose thin-lipped mouth was contorted into a grin of fear and terror, and from under whose body spread a sinister stain that had soaked into the light carpet.

Peter stared at that dead thing with shrinking eyes. It was old Harvey Slade—there was no doubt of that. The thin face and shining bald head were unmistakable, and the manner of his death had been shocking. A feeling or sick revulsion came over him as he saw the handle of the knife that still protruded from the dead man's throat, and for a second the room swam dizzily. He turned and leaned against the doorpost breathing quickly; closing his eyes for a moment to shut out that horrible sight. And then as he opened them again, suddenly and without warning, all the lights went out!

Peter felt his breath leave his lungs in a gasp at the sudden shock. In a momentary panic he swung round, groping blindly for the door. It was bad enough in that room with the lights on, but in the dark… He almost ran into the hall, but the light here had gone out, too, and he paused irresolutely. And then close behind him he heard the sound of soft breathing. Someone was there in the darkness—almost within arm's length of him. He put out his hands, and they touched rough cloth, and then flesh. He heard a low exclamation—a sharp hiss of indrawn breath, and then something crashed down on his head, and the surrounding blackness rushed into his brain and engulfed his senses…

The man who had struck him replaced the spanner in his pocket and flashed the white ray of a torch on the motionless body of his victim. Stooping, he turned Peter over, and gave a little grunt of surprise as he saw his face.

"Now, who the deuce are you?" he muttered, and then: "All right, Lola, the coast is clear."

From the direction of the staircase came the faintest sound of a suppressed sob. A soft, light footstep advanced over the thick carpet, and into the circle of light thrown by the torch in the man's hand, came a girl—a dim figure, slim and graceful, with a white face and terror-laden eyes.

113

"You haven't—you haven't—" She evidently feared to complete the sentence, but her wide, troubled eyes looked at her companion questioningly.

He shook his head.

"I've only put him to sleep for a few minutes," he whispered. "Come on —let's get away from here as quickly as we can."

"Who is it?" She moved nearer, peering down at Peter's motionless form.

"I haven't the least idea," said the man with the torch. "Haven't you seen him before?"

"No." She laid her hand on his arm, and one of her gloves which she had been carrying fell unnoticed to the floor. "He— he isn't a —a detective, is he?"

"I shouldn't think so," replied the other impatiently. "He doesn't look like one. I only caught a glimpse of him from the top of the staircase when he came in, and while he was in the study I crept down and pulled out the fuses. For heaven's sake, don't let us waste any more time. Come along!"

He took her by the arm and led her over to the front door. On the threshold the girl hesitated and looked back. Her eyes rested for a moment fearfully on the entrance to the room in which the dead thing which had once been a man lay grinning up at the ceiling. And then, at an impatient word from her companion, she turned and followed him into the night.

A minute passed— two—and then from the shadows of the hall came a crouching shape. It tiptoed forward, glancing uneasily over its stooping shoulders. Reaching the side of Peter Lake, it bent down and fumbled about his unconscious body...

*　　*　　*　　*

Alone in the darkness and the silence, Peter stirred uneasily and opened his eyes. His head ached dully, and the blackness

114

around him seemed to be pressing in on all sides—a palpable and material weight.

Memory came back with a sudden rush, and he sat up with difficulty, groaning and rubbing his head. He was in the act of scrambling to his feet when he heard the sound of wheels on gravel and the rhythmic throbbing of an engine. A car was coming up the drive, and even as he staggered unsteadily towards the door, it stopped with a squeal of brakes, and there came the muttering of voices.

"Great Scott," thought Peter in dismay, "are there any more of them in this business?"

There were, apparently, four more, anyway, for the open doorway suddenly became blocked with men—big men, two of whom held in their hands electric torches. The foremost uttered a sharp exclamation as his light fell upon the swaying, dishevelled figure of Peter, and he advanced and grabbed him by his arm.

"Anything happened 'ere?" he growled in a hard voice.

Peter had an insane desire to laugh.

"Anything happened?" he echoed shakily and saw for the first time that two of the newcomers were in uniform. "I'm damn sure that very little more could happen."

At the sound of his voice a police constable came forward and peered at him closely.

"Why, if it ain't Dr. Lake!" he cried in surprise. "I thought I knew yer voice, sir. What are you doing here?"

"You know this man, Verney?" snapped the authoritative voice of the man who was gripping Peter's arm.

"Yes, sir," replied Verney. "It's Dr. Lake from the village."

"Humph!" said the hard voice, and Peter felt the fingers that gripped him relax a little. "Well, perhaps Dr. Lake from the village will explain what he's doing here covered in mud and with all the lights out."

Peter hesitated, and the other went on:

"I'm Detective-Inspector Bullot from Scotland Yard."

For a moment Peter had a wild idea that the whole thing was a nightmare.

"From Scotland Yard?" he repeated in amazement. "Then what the deuce are you doing here? How did you know that anything had happened?"

"I'll hear your story first, if you don't mind," broke in the inspector. "I can tell you mine later, if necessary."

Peter pulled himself together and proceeded to give a brief account of all that occurred since he had sought shelter in the telephone-box and had the satisfaction of an attentive audience. Only once was he interrupted, and this was when the Yard man barked an order to one of the policemen.

"See if you can do anything about these lights," he said. "We can't go groping about in the dark. Sorry. Go on, Doctor!"

Peter finished his story and, as he concluded, the lights came on with a flicker.

"That's better," grunted the inspector, a heavy-jowled man with a grey wisp of a moustache. "What was wrong, Verney?"

"Main fuses pulled, that's all, sir," reported the constable from the back of the staircase.

Inspector Bullot grunted again.

"Did you see or hear anything of the girl?" he asked and Peter shook his head.

"I didn't have time to see or hear very much," he replied. "What I did see was quite enough to be going on with."

"You mean the dead man?" The inspector rubbed his chin. "We had better go and have a look at him. Which room did you say it was—the second one?"

Peter pointed to the half-open door, and the inspector went over to it. Before crossing the threshold, he looked back. "Archer, take Verney and make a thorough search of the house. See if you can find any traces of the woman Dr. Lake mentioned. You, Jackson," he nodded to the third man who was still standing by the open front door, "remain on guard here in the hall."

While he was speaking, Peter happened to glance down at the floor, and it was at this moment that he saw the glove that the girl had dropped. Stooping, he picked it up.

"This proves that there was a woman here, anyway," he remarked.

Inspector Bullot came quickly to his side and almost snatched the glove from his hand.

"M'yes." He looked at it, held it to his nose, sniffed twice, and put it carefully in his pocket. "We'll go into that later," he said.

He entered the death room, and following him, Peter watched him from a doorway as he bent over the body.

"H'm! Nasty business!" he muttered, and then looking up quickly: "You're prepared to identify this as Mr. Slade, the owner of the house?"

"I am," said Peter. "There's no doubt about that."

"You didn't make any examination, I suppose?" The inspector's eyes returned to the body. "No, of course you didn't. You didn't have time before the lights went out. We must get hold of the police-surgeon. I'd like to know approximately what time this man met his death."

"I can tell you that roughly," said Peter and, with the Scotland Yard man's permission, made a hasty examination of the body. "He hasn't been dead very long," he announced when he had finished this unpleasant task. "About an hour and a half."

"Then it was probably his screams you heard from the drive," said the inspector, scratching at the grey smear of his moustache. "It's a queer business—a deuced queer business!"

"Look here!" said Peter, putting into words the curiosity that had been consuming him. "How did you get here? I mean—how did you know there was anything wrong?"

The inspector looked at him steadily, and it was a long time before he answered.

"That's the queer part of the business, Dr. Lake," he said at length. "I don't see any reason why I shouldn't tell you. We were told at Scotland Yard that this crime was going to be committed."

Peter's face was expressive of his amazement.

"Told?" he repeated blankly.

Inspector Bullot nodded.

"A letter was delivered by special messenger at nine o'clock this evening," he went on. "I've got it here." He put his hand into his breast-pocket and took out a bulky wallet, and from it a single sheet of paper.

The message it contained was typewritten and very brief.

"To the Chief Commissioner,
     New Scotland Yard.
Sir,
    If you send someone to 'Five Trees' near Higher Wicklow, the home of Mr. Harvey Slade, at eleven o'clock tonight, they'll find a dead man. The reason for the murder will be worth looking into.
'Mr. K.'"

Peter read the message twice and frowned.

"Who the deuce is 'Mr. K.'?" he asked.

Inspector Bullot refolded the paper and put it back into his pocketbook.

"Who is 'Mr. K.'?" he repeated softly. "I should very much like to know that, Dr. Lake—I should like to know that very much indeed!"

CHAPTER 3

The Seeker

In the narrow grimy streets behind Tottenham Court Road, and farther afield in the slums and alleys of Deptford and Netting Dale, they spoke of Mr. K. with hard eyes and an ugly snarl. None of them had ever seen him, or knew what he looked like, but they all hated him. Tired-eyed and dishevelled women, whose men had been taken away in long police cars, nursed vengeance in their hearts, and convicts in the stone quarries at Dartmoor cursed him below their breath as they worked under the watchful eyes of the warders. For Mr. K. was the king of all 'noses'—a police informer in excelsis.

The first of what was destined to be a long series of typewritten slips had reached Scotland Yard eighteen months previously and concerned one Lew Andronsky, a Polish Jew. There had been a big jewel robbery at a shop in Bond Street. The night watchman had suffered severe injuries to his head and had died in hospital a week later.

There was no clue to the murder until Mr. K.'s neat little letter came into the hands of Superintendent Robert Budd. That fat and lethargic official was at first inclined to treat it with the scepticism that such communications deserve, for Scotland Yard looks askance at anonymous letters.

The Assistant Commissioner, however, thought otherwise and ordered that the information should be acted on. He proved to be right, for Lew Andronsky was taken in his sleep at the place mentioned and sufficient evidence was found in his room to convict him ten times over. Some of the stolen jewellery was discovered but the bulk never came to light. Andronsky swore that he had parted with it but he could only give a vague account of where and to whom. According to his story the man in the car had been masked, and the deal had taken place at the side of a country road late at night. Andronsky was found guilty and duly hanged, his last words as he walked from his cell to the gallows being curses against the unknown squealer who had brought about his downfall.

Al Dane, the bank robber, little 'Bud' Smith, Jack Ricketts, and a host of others, in the months that followed all owed their varying sentences to the information received at Scotland Yard over the signature 'Mr. K.'

The existence of this mysterious individual leaked out and stirred up bitter resentment among the criminal classes. There was not one of them, from the petty sneak thief to his bigger brother, who would not cheerfully have torn Mr. K. to pieces if they had had the slightest idea who he was. But he kept himself well hidden. Except for his letters to the police, he gave no tangible evidence that he was alive. And the police knew no more about him than anyone else. He was nothing; an initial at the foot of a typewritten slip, that was all.

Peter Lake heard most of this from Inspector Bullot and listened in wonderment. The whole thing was so divorced from reality, so like a chapter from the many sensational stories he had read, that he found it difficult to believe—until there came into his vision that sprawling shape by the side of the big desk.

"We tried to telephone the local police here," said Bullot, "as soon as we got the letter. But we couldn't get through. The line had been cut a hundred yards away from the station."

He turned towards the door as the constable and the plainclothes man came in.

"Well?" he asked. "Found anything?"

"There are traces in a room upstairs on the first landing that bear out Dr. Lake's story about the woman, sir," said Archer. "There's an extension telephone up there from the main telephone in the hall and the wire has been cut."

"That's where she must have phoned from—" began Peter, and the inspector nodded sharply.

"It doesn't matter at the moment where she phoned from," he interrupted. "Are there any signs of her?"

Archer shook his head.

"No, sir," he replied. "There's no woman in this house. There 'as been though. That room upstairs smells of perfume."

"We know there has been," snapped Bullot irritably, "we've got her glove."

He frowned and twisted his lower lip between his finger and thumb.

"One of you had better take the car and go and rouse the divisional surgeon," he said. "You go, Verney, you know the district. Jackson'll drive you."

The constable saluted and went out. Bullot, with his brows still drawn together, looked at Peter.

"This man, Slade," he said. "Did he live here alone?"

Peter shook his head.

"No," he answered. "He had an elderly man and his wife to look after him."

"Then where are they?" growled Bullot. "You sure there's nobody in the house except ourselves, Archer?"

"Positive, sir," replied the plainclothes man.

"Curious," muttered the inspector. "Where can they have got to?" He looked at his watch. "If they'd had the evening off, they'd have got back now. It's nearly one."

Peter began to realize that he was tired, and that the blow on his head had left it aching rather unpleasantly.

"If you don't want me anymore," he said, "I'd like to be getting home. I've had quite enough for one evening."

Bullot looked at him uncertainly, and then nodded grudgingly.

"Yes, I don't think we want you any more at present," he said. "We can always find you when we do."

He began to move about the room, peering at the furniture and fingering the papers on the desk. Peter said good night, to which the inspector responded with a grunt, and made his way out into the hall. The rain had ceased, but it had cooled the air and he shivered a little as he walked down the drive. It was very dark, and as he got to the gates leading out into the road, he remembered the green fountain pen which he had picked up after his argument with the big man. In the general excitement he had forgotten all about it.

He felt in the jacket pocket in which he had slipped it, but it was no longer there! He stopped just inside the gates and searched in all his pockets, but there was no sign of the pen. It must have been taken from him while he had been unconscious. He was half-minded to go back and tell the inspector about it, but he was very tired, and weariness won. He would telephone first thing in the morning; delay could make very little difference.

He let himself into his small house with a sigh of relief and, going into the kitchen, put the kettle on for a cup of tea. While it was boiling, he undressed and got into a dressing gown. It seemed to him that a vast amount of time had elapsed since he had set out for the Arlingtons', and yet it was only the matter of a few hours.

He smoked a cigarette while the tea brewed and was glad to find that his headache had almost gone. The walk home in the cold air had done it good. He drank his tea and went up to bed. His last waking thought as he snuggled his head into the pillow was of the girl whose voice over the telephone had been the introduction to his evening's adventures…

He awoke suddenly with an uncomfortable feeling that something was wrong. His training had schooled him into passing from sleep to wakefulness without the usual intermediate state, and he sat up alert and watchful. But no sound greeted his straining ears. What had wakened him? What was now giving him that uneasy feeling that he was no longer alone?

He peered into the darkness, but he could neither hear, nor see anything. At his side his watch ticked with apparently unusual loudness, and he was just going to reach over to the little bedside table for it and his torch, which he always kept there, when the gentle pad of feet became audible once more. They ceased and were followed by the rustle of clothes near the foot of the bed.

Cautiously, and without making a sound, Peter reached out for his torch. His fingers closed round it and bringing it round so that the lens pointed at the spot where he judged the unknown to be, Peter pressed the button. A blinding sword blade of light cut the darkness and focused on a crouching shape that was bending over the oak chest on which he had put his clothes. Peter heard a startled gasp and a scurry of feet as the surprised burglar made for the door, and then with a single bound he was out of bed. He caught the intruder just as he was vanishing through the door, and dragging him back, reached up and switched on the light.

His captive, a small roughly-clad man with a cloth cap pulled over his eyes, struggled furiously, but he could not break Peter's grip.

"Now," said Peter grimly, "let's have a look at you, my friend!"

He jerked off the cloth cap and then stared in amazement.

The light glinted on golden hair—two wide, frightened eyes looked up at him...

"Gosh!" exclaimed Peter still staring. "Who are you, what are you doing here?"

The burglar was a girl!

CHAPTER 4

The Big Man

The girl stared up at the astonished Peter with an expression of fear and horror, and then with a sudden movement tried to wrench her arm free from his grasp.

"Oh, no, you don't!" breathed Peter softly, and tightened his fingers. "It's not going to be as easy as that."

Without letting go his hold he went over to the door, shut it, and turned the key.

"Now," he said, slipping the key into the pocket of his pyjama jacket, "we can have a nice quiet little chat."

He pulled on a dressing gown and perched himself on the side of the bed.

"Sit down," he went on, nodding towards a chair by the fireplace. "Make yourself at home."

"What—what are you going to do?"

The low husky voice was appealing, but she made no effort to move from her position by the door.

"It's more a question of what you are going to do." said Peter, and then as she remained silent: "I think I'm entitled to some sort of an explanation, don't you?"

The wide eyes—he noticed they were of a peculiar shade of blue that was almost violet—flickered uneasily; the tip of a pink tongue slid over scarlet lips, but the girl made no reply.

"You know it's not usual to wake up at half-past three in the morning and find a visitor like you in one's room," said Peter conversationally; "in fact, it's distinctly unusual. Who are you, and what's the great idea?"

"Does it matter who I am?"

Her eyes were no longer clouded with fear, but the shakiness of her voice betrayed her unease. Peter, watching her, decided that she was pretty—very pretty—and his interest grew. The rough tweed coat and shapeless flannel trousers she wore enhanced rather than concealed the slimness of her figure. Not at all the kind of burglar one would expect to find in the house at half-past three in the morning.

"I think it matters a lot, under the circumstances," he said slowly. "What I really ought to do instead of sitting here talking is to send for the police—"

"Oh, please don't do that!" The frightened look came back to her eyes and her face whitened. "I've done no harm."

"Only committed burglary, that's all," said Peter a little sarcastically. "A mere nothing."

She bit her lip and her fingers fumbled with the lapel of her jacket.

"You really are rather cool, you know," he went on. "You break into my house, and when you're caught calmly say you've done no harm."

"Neither have I," she said quickly. "I haven't stolen anything. I didn't come to steal anything."

"Then what did you come for?" he broke in.

She hesitated a moment, and then to Peter's surprise she went over to the chair and sat down.

"I came on a matter of life and death," she said seriously.

In the pocket of his dressing gown Peter's hand came in contact with a packet of cigarettes. Mechanically he brought it out, put a cigarette between his lips, and reached over to the little table by his bed for the matches.

"I'd like a cigarette, too, please," said the girl, holding out her hand.

Peter gave her one, found the matches and lit both hers and his own. Sitting once more on the edge of the bed, the humour of the situation suddenly burst on him, and he chuckled.

"What are you laughing at?"

She looked at him wonderingly with the cigarette halfway to her lips.

125

"I'm laughing because the whole thing strikes me as being funny," said Peter. "This is the first time I've enjoyed the thrill of being burgled, and instead of adopting the proper course laid down for all respectable householders and handing the burglar over to the tender mercies of the police, I entertain her with a cigarette."

She smiled—rather an anaemic attempt, but still a smile. Peter discovered that she had a most attractive dimple at the corner of her mouth.

"You know I'm not a burglar," she said.

He raised his eyebrows.

"Well, not an ordinary burglar," she added hastily. "I'll admit that I've no right to be here."

"I'm glad you appreciate the enormity of your offence," said Peter, and this time she laughed outright.

It was a pleasant sound—at least Peter thought so—and added to his mental catalogue of her attractions two rows of small, even and very white teeth.

"I'm afraid I'm too much of a hardened criminal to allow it to weigh very heavily on my conscience," she retorted.

The fear had gone completely from her eyes, and in its place had appeared a slight twinkle. Peter felt his heart warming towards this girl in spite of the—to say the least of it—unconventional situation in which he had met her. She exhaled a subtle something which for want of a better word, he put down as charm, that made it seem as though he had known her for a very long time.

"Suppose you tell me all about it?" he suggested. "The reason for all this, I mean." He nodded towards her masculine attire. "I'm presuming, of course, that it's not a habit of yours to walk about dressed like that and break into people's houses."

"I didn't break in," she said. "The kitchen window was open."

126

Peter remembered that he had forgotten to perform his usual rounds before going to bed.

"But I take it you don't usually enter people's houses by any window you happen to see open?" he remarked.

She grew suddenly serious.

"No, but on this occasion—as I said—it is a matter of life and death," she replied. She inhaled deeply at her cigarette and threw the end into the fireplace. "I wonder if I can trust you?" she said.

Peter returned her gaze steadily.

"I think you can," he answered. "Why not try?"

She was silent for quite a long time, and Peter felt that she was taking stock of him.

"Will you treat what I have to say in strict confidence?" she said at last.

He hesitated. Supposing she told him something that it was his duty to pass on to the police? He knew nothing about her, and besides, he felt sure that it was she who had been in that house of death at the time old Harvey Slade had been killed. He had refrained from letting her know it, but he had recognized her voice directly she had spoken as the voice of the girl on the telephone.

She saw his hesitation and guessed the reason for it.

"I know nothing about the murder," she said, and Peter's face must have expressed his surprise, for she went on: "Oh, yes, I know you were in the house tonight, and I know what you found there. But I don't know who killed Slade or why he was killed."

"Do you know 'Mr. K.'?"

The question was past Peter's lips before he could check it, and the effect on the girl was electrical. Her calmness slipped from her like water from a greasy plate. The look of fear came back to her eyes, and she paled to the lips.

127

"What—what do you know of Mr. K.?" she breathed huskily.

"Nothing at all," said Peter. "I never heard of him until tonight."

He stopped abruptly and stared at the door. Was it just fancy or had he heard a sound outside in the passage? The girl in the chair followed the direction of his eyes, and her lips parted to speak, but with a quick gesture Peter stopped her and rose to his feet. He had not been mistaken. The handle of the door was softly turning! Somebody outside was trying it to see if it was locked.

In two strides Peter was across the room.

"Who's there?" he called sharply.

The answer to his question was startling. There was a sudden crash and the door bulged under the weight of a heavy body!

With a sharp cry the girl sprang to her feet and stood with horrified eyes, her hand at her throat, staring at the creaking woodwork.

"What the hell—" began Peter angrily, and then, with a splintering, rending sound, the lock gave and the door flew open.

"Don't move either of you!" snarled a harsh voice and a man came in out of the darkness of the passage.

Peter saw the light glint on the blue nose of an automatic, and his fingers relaxed their grip on the chair he had hastily picked up.

The second visitor of that night was the big man he had nearly knocked out in the drive at 'Five Trees'!

CHAPTER 5

Superintendent Budd Arrives

The huge figure filled the doorway; a great mountain of living flesh. The abnormally small head set upon a bull neck above the big shoulders swayed gently from side to side like a snake about to strike. Indeed, there was something curiously reptilian about the whole face. The eyes were small and set closely to the round button of a nose; the mouth a twisted red streak that showed up vividly against the grey-white of the skin, was cruel and sensual. On the left cheek—Peter saw this with satisfaction—was a livid bruise.

"Get over there—against the wall." The voice, devoid now of its previous harshness, was low and gentle like the soft hiss of escaping steam. "There is a fresh clip of cartridges in this little thing, and if you don't do as I tell you, you'll get them all—equally divided between you."

Peter's hands clenched until the nails dug into the palms. A fierce longing to hit this great swollen thing took possession of him, but the sight of the unwavering automatic suggested discretion. It was useless putting up a fight against that. With an almost imperceptible shrug of his shoulders, he backed towards the wall the other had indicated.

"That was very wise of you," said the big man gently. "Second thoughts are always best. Now,"—he looked from Peter to the terrified girl—"which of you has it?"

Peter stole a quick glance at his companion. Her eyes were fixed in a stare of horror on the newcomer, and she was breathing in little, short, irregular gasps.

"Come on!" The gentle hissing voice changed to a snarl. "One of you has it—which one?"

"Has what?" said Peter.

129

"The pen!" snapped the big man. "I had it in my hand when I ran into you in the drive."

Peter heard the girl draw in her breath sharply, but without taking his eyes off the man with the pistol he said:

"Which pen?"

"The green pen," said the big man, and his small, beady eyes were full of menace. "It's no good trying to pretend you don't know what I'm talking about. I know you've got it!"

"Then you know a damn sight more than I do," said Peter coolly.

The thin lips drew back in a mirthless grin, showing a row of broken discoloured teeth.

"Takin' that line, eh?" he snarled viciously. "Well, you can cut it out as soon as you like. You've got that pen, and I want it, so hand it over and look slippy about it or it'll be the worse for you!" He waved the muzzle of the automatic threateningly.

"Is it your pen?" asked Peter to gain time, his brain working hastily to find some way out of this unpleasant situation.

"Never mind whose pen it is," snapped the big man angrily. "It isn't yours, anyway, and this is none of your business. If you take my advice, you'll keep out of it: you know what happened to Harvey Slade?"

"I do," replied Peter grimly.

"Well," said the other, "that's liable to happen again to anyone who butts in on this game."

"Thanks for the tip," said Peter. "Were you responsible for that devilish crime?"

"I wasn't," said the big man curtly.

Peter looked at him steadily.

"Perhaps it was 'Mr. K.'," he suggested.

A startled expression flashed for a second in the other's face, and then he laughed, a cracked, unpleasant sound that was completely divorced from mirth.

"Perhaps it was," he answered, "and perhaps it wasn't. I didn't come here to answer questions, anyhow, and I don't propose to stay here all night, so hand over that pen and I'll go."

"If you intend stopping until you get that," said Peter, "you'll stop here forever."

"Oh, will I?" hissed the big man, and his eyes narrowed until they almost completely disappeared. "We'll see about that!" He advanced two steps and thrust the pistol forward. "Now," he grated. "I'll give you until I count three to hand over that pen, after that I shall shoot!"

"I can save you the trouble of counting at all," said Peter calmly. "I haven't got the pen."

The face before him twisted into an ugly expression.

"I'm not bluffing—" began the big man.

"I'm not bluffing either," snapped Peter. "I tell you I haven't got the pen."

"Then what have you done with it?" The small head turned slowly. "Have you given it to—her?" He looked at the girl balefully.

Peter shook his head.

"What makes you so certain I ever had it?" he asked.

For the first time he saw an expression of doubt come into the other's face.

"I lost it in the drive," he muttered. "I know that, and when I went back to look for it, it had gone—"

"That may be true," agreed Peter, "but it doesn't follow that I was the person who picked it up."

"You were there—" began the big man, but Peter interrupted him.

"So were a good many people," he said. "The people who slugged me, and afterwards the police!"

"The police!" There was something very like fear in the tone. "They haven't got it, have they?"

"I don't know who's got it," said Peter truthfully and a little irritably. "I only know I haven't. What are you making such a fuss about, anyway? It was only a fountain pen; you can get another exactly like it for ten and sixpence."

The other took no notice. He seemed to be thinking rapidly. "Who slugged you?" he asked after a slight pause. "What was he like?"

"I don't know," replied Peter. "If you'd been hit as hard as I was you wouldn't have known either." And then his anger got the better of him. "Look here," he said, "I'm sick of all these questions, and I'm sick of you and this melodrama stuff. Put that pistol away and clear out."

The big man's pasty face flushed.

"That's enough of that unless you want to get hurt," he snarled. "I'll go when I'm ready and don't forget I've got the whip-hand!" He tapped his pistol meaningfully. "How do I know that you haven't been lying? How do I know that you haven't got that pen hidden somewhere all the time?"

Peter thought rapidly. How was it possible to turn the tables on this unpleasant adversary?

"Lost your tongue?" snapped the big man impatiently, "or are you trying to think out some more lies? I know you've got that pen, so why not be sensible and hand it over?"

"Supposing I give you the pen," said Peter slowly as an idea occurred to him, "will you clear out?"

The expression of the other's face became eager.

"Directly I get that pen I'll go," he answered.

"Then I suppose I'd better give it to you," said Peter with a shrug of his shoulders, and walked over to the oak chest on which his clothes lay.

A startled exclamation came from the girl.

"Don't do that," she began and the big man swung round on her quickly.

132

"You shut up!" he snarled and advanced a step towards Peter. "Come on, hand it over!"

Peter, with his heart beating quickly, picked up his dinner jacket. He made a pretence of feeling in the pocket and then suddenly and without warning flung the jacket full in the big man's face. Taken completely by surprise he staggered back, firing wildly as he did so. The shots, however, whistled harmlessly past Peter and buried themselves in the wall, and the next second, he had leaped forward, knocked the gun from the other's hand, and launched himself upon him.

They both crashed heavily to the floor, the big man fighting like a tiger. But Peter was uppermost and held his advantage. With a stream of oaths, the other sought for his throat, but Peter gripped his wrists and tore them away. Together they rolled over and over towards the open door and landed with a thud against the jamb. It was Peter's head that came in contact with the wood and the impact dazed him. His grip loosened and, taking advantage of the fact, the big man threw him off and scrambled to his feet. Before Peter could recover, he was running heavily down the passage.

Peter went in pursuit and caught his quarry as he reached the head of the staircase. He dodged a swinging blow to his jaw and retaliated by a short-arm left hook which caught the big man under the heart and made him gasp. The next second, he had closed with Peter and they went reeling against the banisters. Peter would easily have got the better of him then, if his foot hadn't slipped. As it was, he lost his balance, and the pair of them went crashing down the staircase to land in a heap in the hall below.

Peter felt the breath leave his body in one enormous gasp as the big man's full weight descended on his stomach. His senses whirled dizzily and as from a long distance he heard an irregular knocking. Dazedly he felt the weight across him suddenly removed and then, as he recovered his breath, the knocking developed into a thunderous tattoo on the front door.

He heard the thudding of feet and the bang of a door from the back as he scrambled shakily to his feet and stood leaning against the newel-post. Rat-tat-tat! The knocking came again louder and more insistent. Peter pulled himself together. Who the deuce was this? Some more of them? He hesitated. Perhaps it would be just as well not to open that door. He didn't feel like tackling anybody else at the moment. The knocking was repeated and he heard the rattle of the letterbox as a hand raised the flap.

"Hello, there!" called a deep voice. "Anything wrong?"

"Who are you?" said Peter, feeling along the wall for the light switch.

"I'm Superintendent Budd from Scotland Yard," answered the voice. "If that's Dr. Lake I want to see him."

Peter heard a little gasp of dismay at his elbow, and a hand checked him from turning on the light. The girl had crept down the stairs and was now standing beside him in the hall.

"Don't open the door—yet," she breathed in his ear and, as her soft lips brushed his cheek, Peter felt an unusual thrill surge through him. She thrust the big man's gun into his hand and then she was gone, leaving behind the faintest trace of an elusive perfume. Against his better judgment Peter let her go.

"Alright," he called to the man outside the door. "Half a second and I'll let you in."

He waited, pretending to fumble with the chain, until he concluded that the girl had had time to get out through the back, and then switching on the light he opened the door.

A portly figure entered, and Peter saw the lights of a small car at the end of the little path by the gate.

Mr. Robert Budd took in his dishevelled appearance in one apparently lazy glance and his eyes half closed.

134

"Dear me, Dr. Lake," he said gently, "you appear to have been having a rough time!"

CHAPTER 6

Death in the Garden

"A big fat man with a small head," remarked Mr. Budd slowly. "H'm! Might almost be a description of me except that I haven't got a small head." He shook it gently as though to emphasize its size. "No, I can't recollect any known criminal like that. He's a new one on me."

He was sitting in Peter's shabby little consulting-room sipping the hot tea that at his suggestion Peter had hastily brewed. In the cold grey light of early morning that came in through the window his big heavy face looked old and tired. Peter attributed this to the fact that the stout detective had been up all night, being unaware that it was Mr. Robert Budd's habitual expression. He had just finished an account of his night's adventures—an account that was true and unembellished, with the exception of one important detail. He had very carefully omitted all mention of the girl in the flannel trousers and sports jacket. Just why he had done this he would have had some difficulty in explaining. Possibly it was just an innate sense of chivalry which is not nearly so dead as the present generation likes to believe.

Mr. Budd gulped down the remains of his second cup of tea and crossed one fat leg over the other.

"This is a funny business all round," he murmured with a prodigious yawn balancing the empty cup and saucer on a broad knee. "A very funny business."

"It hasn't struck me as particularly humorous," said Peter dryly.

'Rosebud'—as he was called by his friends and foes alike, partly because of his name, but mostly because of his passion for roses of all kinds—looked at his new acquaintance with sleepy eyes.

"Hasn't it now?" he said, and his voice sounded a little sorrowful, as though he was rather disappointed. "Hasn't it? Well, well, p'r'aps we don't look at things in the same way. Now there are several things about this business that strike me as remarkably funny." He paused, and with an effort set the cup and saucer down on the floor beside his chair. "I'll tell you some of 'em."

He settled himself more comfortably with a protesting creak from the chair.

"One," he went on counting on the fingers of a stubby hand: "Why did Slade send his servants away? They're not in the house and they haven't come back, so I conclude that he sent 'em away. That's joke number one. Joke number two is, who wrote that letter to the Yard sayin' there was goin' to be a murder?"

"Mr. K., whoever he is," said Peter.

"No, he didn't," contradicted the stout superintendent decisively, or as near decisively as it was possible for him to get. "I've seen that letter, an' I've compared it with the others by 'Mr. K.', and I'm willin' to bet he never wrote it."

"How can you be so certain?" asked Peter. "It was typewritten—"

"I know it was typewritten," broke in Mr. Budd. "Even Bullot could see that. But it wasn't typewritten with the same machine an' it wasn't typewritten on the same paper."

"I don't see that that's conclusive," said Peter. "He could easily have used a different machine and paper."

The Rosebud eyed him pityingly.

"He could but he didn't," he said gently. "Because as well as what I've just told you, he spelt 'commissioner' wrong and 'chief' wrong."

"Yes, I noticed that," Peter nodded.

"Did you?" said Mr. Budd approvingly. "Then you're a better detective than Bullot—not that that's much of a compliment. Well, Mr. K. never made a spelling mistake before an' he's always sent his letters to the Chief Commissioner. No, you can take it from me that feller 'K.' never wrote it."

Peter frowned.

"Why should anyone else write it?" he demanded.

The stout superintendent started to shrug his shoulders, found the effort too great, and stopped halfway.

"I don't know for certain," he answered. "P'r'aps it was because they wanted to make sure that the police 'ud act on the information, an' p'r'aps it was for another reason." He suddenly opened his eyes very wide. "How well did you know this feller Slade?" he asked.

"I didn't know him at all—except by sight," answered Peter. "I've seen him once or twice in the village. That's all."

"H'm!" grunted the Rosebud, lapsing once more into his previous lethargic state. "Well, whoever killed him saved the country a bit o' money."

Peter looked surprised.

"What do you mean?" he asked curiously.

"If he hadn't been killed, he'd have got fifteen years," replied Mr. Budd. "We found enough evidence up at that house to convict him ten times over."

"Of what?" asked the astonished Peter.

"Fencing and blackmail," was the laconic answer.

"Great Scott!" exclaimed Peter. "Old Slade?"

"Old Slade," repeated the stout man. "I told you this was a funny business, an' one of the funniest things about it is the girl who phoned you. I'd like to know who she is and why Slade locked her up."

His eyes sought Peter's as he spoke and they were no longer lazy. Peter shifted uneasily and felt himself flushing. He had an uncomfortable feeling that Mr. Budd was aware that the girl had been there that night,

"She couldn't have had anything to do with the murder," he said hastily. "Slade was alive when he locked her in—"

"He was alive when he locked her in," said the Rosebud, "but was he alive when somebody let her out?" He was still watching Peter steadily. "Somebody let her out, you know. She couldn't have got out by the window because it was screwed up, an' she couldn't have turned the key herself because it was on the outside of the door. An' she wasn't there when Bullot arrived, so I deduce that somebody let her out."

He waited, but Peter remained silent.

"Did the somebody who let her out kill Slade," Mr. Budd went on, "or was Slade already dead when the somebody arrived? It's all very interestin' and peculiar, and the most interestin' thing about it is why that feller who came here is so anxious about that green pen." He nodded several times, and then went off at a tangent. "Do you use scent, Dr. Lake?"

The question took Peter completely by surprise. It was so unexpected.

"Er—no—why?" he stammered.

"Thought I smelt scent when I came in," said Mr. Budd. "If you don't use it, it must have been my imagination. Imagination's one of my strong points. I'm always imagining things. F'r instance, this scent I thought I smelt was just like the scent that girl left behind in that room at 'Five Trees.'"

So, he knew, thought Peter in dismay; knew that the girl had been there that night in spite of the fact that he hadn't mentioned it. The sleepy looking eyes and lazy manner were just a blind concealing a particularly alert brain. Still Peter decided he had no direct proof, and he wasn't going to be trapped into admitting that the girl had been there.

"Your imagination must be very vivid indeed," he said as coolly as he could. "I can't smell any scent."

"I can't—now," said the stout superintendent and hoisted himself with difficulty to his feet. "What sort of a garden have you got here?" he asked.

Peter was getting a little bewildered at these sudden changes of subject.

"Nothing very much," he answered.

"I'd like to see it," said Mr. Budd. "I'm fond of gardens. Horticulture's my hobby. Besides, that big feller, when he escaped, may have left some interestin' traces."

He moved over to the door, and Peter followed puzzling over the reason for the sudden desire to view his small scrap of land. He did not believe for a moment that the detective's explanation was the real one. Leading the way along the passage and through the tiny kitchen he opened the back door.

"There you are," he said. "There's the garden, such as it is." Mr. Budd looked slowly about him.

"Could be made very nice with a little trouble," he remarked. "Those rose trees want prunin' another year. You'd get better blooms. So, this was the way that feller went—along that path and through the little gate?" He dropped his eyes to the wet gravel at his feet and shook his head. "Curious," he said, "you never told me he was wearin' ladies' shoes!"

Peter followed the direction of his eyes and saw the clear print of a dainty shoe—the cause of Mr. Budd's remark. So that was why he had been so interested in the garden. He had guessed that if the girl had been there, she would leave this way and had hoped to find confirmation of her presence.

"I—" began Peter, and discovered he was speaking to empty air. With surprisingly quick strides for one of his size, Mr. Budd was moving swiftly down the path in the direction of the small gate at the end of the garden.

Peter frowned and went after him wondering what had so suddenly interested him. Halfway along the path he saw.

140

Near the gate was a thick bank of evergreens, and projecting from the massed foliage—a foot!

It was a large foot, and with a rapidly beating heart Peter broke into a run. As he came level with Mr. Budd the stout man stooped and parted the screening branches. The green of the leaves was splashed and mottled with red, and Peter saw the reason as he gazed down at the huddled form that lay in their midst.

It was the big man, and he had died in the same way that Harvey had died—horribly, stabbed in the throat!

CHAPTER 7

The Warning!

The man seated at the wheel of the motionless car looked anxiously along the wide stretch of country road dimly visible in the grey of the dawn and cursed softly below his breath. He was feeling cold and stiff, huddled up among his rugs in the shadowy recesses of the limousine.

Presently the man at the wheel—a little wizened fellow with a yellow pockmarked face, yawned, stretched himself, and producing a cheap packet of cigarettes, lighted one. He inhaled the smoke gratefully and, turning, slid back a window in the glass partition that separated the driving-seat from the interior of the car.

"'Ow much longer d'you think Ledder's going ter be, guv'nor?" he asked, peering through the square aperture.

The man addressed grunted and raised his head.

"How should I know?" he snapped irritably. "The fool ought to have been back by now."

"P'r'aps he's 'ad trouble," said the little man apprehensively.

"Ledder's capable of taking care of himself," growled the other.

"Bit o' bad luck 'is runnin' up against the chap in the drive," muttered the pockmarked man. "If 'e 'adn't done that we'd a got what we was after and bin away by now."

"It was cursed bad management on Ledder's part," retorted the man in the car. "If the sight of old Slade lying there dead hadn't scared him, he'd have been more careful."

His companion shivered.

"I was scared too," he admitted candidly. "An' I only 'eard the scream. Blimey! It was awful, wasn't it?"

The thin lips of the man behind him curled into a contemptuous sneer.

"It didn't upset me," he replied.

"Nuthin' 'ud upset you," said the little man with grudging admiration. "You ain't got no nerves, guv'nor."

"I've got nerves, but I know how to control them, Bilter," was the reply. "It would take more than a scream and the sight of a dead man to scare me into a panic."

Bilter relapsed into silence, puffing at his cigarette.

"I wonder 'oo killed the old beggar?" he said thoughtfully at last.

The thin shoulders of the other hunched into a shrug.

"Does it matter?" he snapped harshly. "Whoever it was, he saved me the trouble. Nothing but death would have parted Slade from his precious pen."

"I 'ope Ledder's succeeded in gettin' it," said Bilter. "Ter think 'e 'ad it in 'is 'and, and then lost it!" He stopped as a thought struck him. "'Ere, I say," he went on, his voice suddenly shrill with anxiety. "Yer don't think 'e's got it and 'e's goin' off with it on his own, do you? He's bin a 'ell of a long time—"

"He wouldn't dare." The words were confident, but the tone of the voice suggested a slight doubt. "He wouldn't dare try and double-cross me."

"Ledder 'ud double-cross the h'angel Gabriel if 'e thought 'e was goin' to get enough out of it," declared Bilter. "An' don't you make no mistake."

The heavy brows of the man in the back drew down over the bridge of his thin pendulous nose. There was something vulture-like about him as he sat there half-crouched in the corner, thinking over the startling suggestion that his companion had put forward.

"I don't think Ledder would risk it even though the prize is a high one," he said at length. "He knows me too well, and he knows that if he did that, I'd get him wherever he went."

Bilter threw away the stub of his cigarette.

"Well, I wish 'e'd 'urry up that's all," he said. "I'm cold and I'm tired and I'm sick of sittin' 'ere."

"I'm tired too, but I'm not making a fuss about it," snarled the other. "You want to live on a bed of roses."

"There ain't bin no bed nor roses about tonight," grumbled the little man. "Me 'eart's in me mouth most of the time."

"I wish it was there now," grated his companion. "Perhaps it would stop you talking. Shut up and shut that window. There's an infernal draught."

Bilter opened his mouth to reply, thought better of it, slammed the sliding window to, and huddled himself up as comfortably as he could in his seat.

The man inside the car drew his rugs closer around and stared out of the side window at the rapidly lightening landscape.

To judge by his face his thoughts were not pleasant ones, for every now and again he scowled, and his lips compressed until they were almost invisible in the grey of his face. It was an evil face, lined and scored and greed showed in the furrows about the nostrils and mouth. And yet the man could not have been so very old for the hair—such of it as could be seen under the broad brim of the soft hat he wore—was jet black.

The minutes passed and presently he stirred, fumbled in his breast pocket and produced a cigar-case. Selecting a cigar and biting off the end with a set of peculiarly white and even teeth, he settled back once more in his corner.

It was Bilter who first heard the sound of the car engine. On the still air of the morning, it came with remarkable clearness long before the car itself was visible, and it woke Bilter from a gentle doze.

He sat up looking along the ribbon of road that stretched ahead with narrowed eyes. He saw the car come round the bend and noticed that it was travelling at good speed.

The sound of the exhaust grew louder, and he saw that the machine was a long low racer, painted black. There was only one occupant, a solitary figure crouched over the wheel.

Without a great deal of interest Bilter watched the car draw nearer, but he suddenly became alert as the low humming roar of the engine dwindled when it was a hundred yards away and the machine began to slow down. With an oath he swung himself out of the driving seat and dropped on to the roadway as the black car slid alongside the standing limousine and came to a halt.

"Stay where you are and don't trouble to pull that gun," ordered a high-pitched voice, and Bilter, whose hand had gone instinctively to his hip pocket, found himself staring blankly into the muzzle of an automatic held in the gloved hand of the driver.

"I'm a very good shot," continued the voice, "so I don't advise you to take any risks. If I have to shoot, I shall shoot to kill."

"What do you want?" began Bilter hoarsely.

"I want to speak to your employer," interrupted the man with the gun. "Open the door and tell him to get out."

With one eye on the gun Bilter moved to obey, but was saved the trouble, for the window slid down and the scowling face of the man inside was thrust through the aperture.

"What's all this?" he demanded harshly.

"Good morning, Mr. Paul Andronsky," greeted the man in the black car pleasantly. "I've just come along to save you wasting your time."

The face of the man addressed as Andronsky went grey, and there was a flicker of fear in his eyes as he stared at the leather-covered head and goggled eyes of the other.

145

"Who are you?" he stammered. "What do you mean?"

"Your brother knew me as 'Mr. K.', and that's as good a name as any other," answered the goggled man calmly.

"Mr. K!" Paul Andronsky's lean jaw dropped and the fear in his eyes deepened to sheer terror. Bilter, his eyes almost starting from his head, muttered a strangled oath.

Mr. K. took no notice of the sensation he had caused.

"Lew Andronsky tried to play me up," he went on still in the same high-pitched obviously disguised voice, "and for that he went to the gallows. Al Dane, Bud Smith, and Jack Ricketts tried the same game, and they, too, suffered in varying degrees."

Paul Andronsky's face flushed, changing from unhealthy grey to an unpleasant liver colour.

"You darned squealer!" he snarled thickly.

"Not at all," said the man in the black car coolly. "I merely used the law to punish them instead of doing so myself, and I can assure you that the law was more lenient than I should have been. But I'm not going to waste time, either discussing or justifying my methods."

His voice changed and there was a menacing note in it that sent a cold shiver through the two men he was addressing:

"Keep out of this Slade business, Andronsky. I know what you're after but you won't get it—neither will Ledder. That green pen, when it's found, belongs to me. I don't know who's got it at the moment, but when I find out it will be the worse for them."

His left hand came up out of the car with a throwing motion and something fell at Bilter's feet.

"It's no good waiting for Ledder," he said. "He won't come back—perhaps you can guess why."

He pressed his foot on the accelerator, and the long black car shot forward and roared away up the road. As the sound of

146

its engine grew less Bilter stooped and picked up the thing at his feet.

"Blimey!" he breathed huskily, and his face was chalk white, for between his shaking fingers was a long-bladed knife, and the steel was wet with blood. He looked at Paul Andronsky, but neither asked whose blood it was—they both knew!

CHAPTER 8

Peter Gets Another Shock

To Peter Lake the three hours following the discovery of the body of the big man were like a particularly unpleasant nightmare. His small house literally buzzed with policemen. Inspector Bullot hastily summoned, arrived breathlessly, held a hurried conference with Mr. Robert Budd, left behind a local inspector and a constable and departed in a whirl of officialdom. The police surgeon, a man from the neighbouring town, came just before the ambulance. He was a brusque man with a staccato manner of speech, and Peter, who had never seen him before, took an instant and intense dislike to him. He rather grudgingly confirmed Peter's diagnosis of the cause of death, promised to drop his report into the station during the morning, and went away with the ambulance and all that remained of the big man.

"He was murdered by the same man who murdered Slade," said Mr. Robert Budd, puffing at an evil-smelling black cigar, which he had extracted from one of the pockets of his capacious waistcoat. "There's no doubt about that. The two killings are identical, except that in Slade's case he left the knife behind."

"Who was the dead man? Did you find out?" asked Peter, and the stout superintendent nodded.

"He was a man called Ledder," he answered. "Beyond that I don't know anything about him, but it won't be very long before I know all about him. There was a letter in his pocket, with his name and address on it and I'm havin' inquiries made." He rolled the cigar from one corner of his mouth to the other. "About this green pen, Dr. Lake," he went on, "are you quite certain that the person who 'coshed' you took it?"

148

"Well, I had it in my pocket at the time and I hadn't got it after," said Peter, "so it seems pretty obvious."

"H'm!" remarked the Rosebud, staring at a corner of the ceiling. "Ledder couldn't have known that, or he wouldn't have taken the trouble to come along here after it. It looks as though more than one person was interested in that pen."

Peter could have assured him definitely on this point, but he kept his mouth shut. Throughout the questions that had been fired at him that morning he had been dreading that Mr. Budd would revert to the presence of the girl and demand an explanation for that telltale footprint on the gravel. He had even been at some pains to think up a good one, but the dreaded question never came. Mr. Budd had apparently forgotten all about the footprint in the stress of more important things.

Again and again, Peter told himself that he was a fool, and something more than a fool to worry about a girl of whom he knew nothing, and had only seen once in his life, and then under circumstances that wanted a lot of explaining.

By suppressing evidence that might be helpful to the police he was laying himself open to a grave charge. The punishment for an accessory after the fact in murder was no light one, and he was risking all this for a pretty face that dimpled rather nicely when it smiled. No, that was not quite true. There was something more in it than that; something about the girl's personality that had reached out and found an answering something in his own. That was the only way he could describe it, and although his brain told him that he was acting like a fool, he could no more have followed its suggestion than he could have flown.

Instinct, which is older, and in certain circumstances, stronger than reason, had the upper hand.

Mr. Budd took his departure at last, leaving Peter hollow-eyed from his sleepless night, to sit down to a frugal lunch prepared by the woman, who came in daily to 'do for him' and sometimes nearly did.

He was just finishing his meal when George Arlington arrived. A tall, readily-smiling man of thirty-six, he radiated cheerfulness.

"What's all this I hear?" he greeted, dropping into a chair and lighting a cigarette. "Battle, murder and sudden death let loose in the village. Tell me all about it."

Peter swallowed a final mouthful of bread and cheese.

"I'll tell you nothing, George," he said. "I'm sick of the whole thing."

His friend eyed him sympathetically.

"Had a gruelling, have you?" he murmured. "You don't look up to much, but you must make an effort, old man. Here's a first-class sensation, with you as the central figure, and I'm longing to hear all the gory details."

Peter groaned and pushed back his chair from the table.

"How did you hear anything about it?" he said.

Arlington smiled—a curious smile that ran up one side of his face, leaving the other in repose.

"I am the possessor of a servant," he replied, "who is better at dishing out news than any newspaper. I heard all about the business at breakfast."

"Then why come and bother me?" demanded Peter impolitely.

"Because you are in possession of the inside information," retorted his friend. "Now, come on, spill the beans, and let's hear all about it."

"Give me a cigarette, then," said Peter, valiantly trying to suppress a yawn and failing. "You're a beastly old slavedriver, George."

Arlington grinned and gave him a cigarette, and Peter, after a preliminary puff, began his story.

His audience was an attentive one, for he listened without interruption. When Peter had finished, he pursed his lips and whistled.

"By Jove, it's a mysterious business!" he remarked. "I wonder what happened to the girl?"

Peter hesitated. He had half a mind to tell his friend about the girl's visit, but he thought better of it and shook his head.

"I couldn't tell you," he said, easing his conscience with the reflection that this was strictly true.

"It seems to me," Arlington continued, "that it's damned lucky for you that you did lose that pen, or have it pinched. Rather unhealthy to have it in one's possession apparently." He flicked the end of his cigarette into the fireplace. "I'd like to know why that fellow—what's his name—"

"Ledder," said Peter and Arlington nodded.

"I'd like to know why he was so keen to get hold of it."

"So would the police," said Peter. "There must be something concealed in that pen of considerable value."

"I agree with you," Arlington wrinkled his brows thoughtfully. "You say this man Slade was a fence? Perhaps he was a miser as well, and the pen shows where he's hidden his money?"

Peter was too tired to offer any suggestions. His eyes felt hot and heavy, through lack of sleep, and he wished George Arlington to Jericho. But George was full of ideas and theories, and he recounted these at great length until Peter could cheerfully have killed him.

However, he went at last, after extricating a promise from Peter to keep him posted with all the latest developments and Peter dragged his weary body upstairs to his bedroom. Dressed as he was, he flung himself on the bed, and with a sigh of relief buried his aching head in the cool pillow.

It must have been late when he awoke, for it was quite dark outside and, looking at his watch, he saw that the time was

151

nearly eleven. But his long sleep had done him good. After a cold bath he went downstairs feeling as fit as a fiddle and ravenously hungry.

He was rummaging about in the pantry in search of food when he thought he heard a sound at the back door. Going out into the little scullery, he stood listening. The sound came again; irregular sobbing breathing, and this time it was accompanied by a frantic scrabbling on the panels.

In two strides Peter was at the door. Pulling back the bolt, he turned the handle, and then, as the door swung open, something fell heavily into his arms. With an exclamation of alarm and surprise, he found himself looking down into the unconscious face of the girl of the previous night!

CHAPTER 9

Lola Marsh's Secret

She lay limply in his arms breathing heavily and at first Peter was afraid that she had been hurt. A second rapid glance, however, reassured him. She had only fainted.

He carried her into the consulting room, laid her down on the shabby little settee, and set to work to bring her round. In a few seconds his efforts were rewarded, for she opened her eyes. He saw the wild fear in them as she started up and laid a soothing hand on her shoulder.

"Keep still for a bit," he said. "You're quite safe."

The terror faded from her face, and as he slipped a cushion behind her head, she sank back against it with a little sigh. Peter stood looking down at her in silence and thought he had never seen anything more lovely. She was dressed this time in a severely-cut costume of black face-cloth, and the sombre hue brought out all the beauty of her hair and skin. The small black hat she had been wearing he had taken off, and realizing that he was still holding it, he set it down on the table. Turning back again, he saw that she was watching him solemnly.

"Feeling better?" he asked.

She nodded.

"What happened?" he went on. "Something frightened you. What was it?"

A shadow of the fear he had seen before returned to her eyes.

"It was the man in the drive," she said in a low voice, and shivered.

Peter stared.

"The man in the drive?" he repeated. "Which drive?"

"The drive at 'Five Trees'," she answered.

"What in the world were you doing there at this time of night?" said Peter in amazement.

"I was going to the house," she replied simply and without hesitation, "and half-way up the drive I ran into him. He had on a leather helmet and goggles, and he started to chase me. I was horribly frightened, and I ran and ran until I found myself near your gate. I thought I'd be safe here—"

Peter ran his fingers through his hair.

"Look here," he suggested. "Suppose you tell me all you know about this extraordinary business. It all seems quite mad to me. I'm like a man who has gone into a theatre in the middle of a play and gets in half-way through the second act. I don't know the plot and,"—he looked at her meaningfully—"I don't know the names of the characters."

"I don't know them all," she said with a faint smile that brought out the dimple again, "but my name's Lola Marsh, if that's what you mean."

"That was partly what I meant, thank you," said Peter, and went on quickly: "I don't want to butt in on something that doesn't concern me, but if there's anything I can do I'd like to help."

The violet blue eyes softened.

"That's rather nice of you, Dr. Lake," she murmured, "particularly after what—after what we did to you." She saw the bewilderment in his face and went on quickly: "It was Jim, my brother, who—who hit you last night at 'Five Trees'."

"Oh, was it?" said Peter grimly.

"He didn't know it was you," said Lola hastily. "I mean we thought you were one of the others."

"I see," said Peter, and frowned. "So, it wasn't you or your brother who took that green pen out of my pocket?"

She shook her head.

154

"Of course, it wasn't," she said. "Otherwise, I shouldn't have come here last night to try and get it. Did you think it was?"

"I naturally thought it was the person who coshed me," said Peter, "because I don't see who else had the chance."

"Somebody may have come in while you were still unconscious—after we had gone," she suggested, and Peter nodded.

"That seems to be a possible explanation," he agreed. "What is there about this pen that makes it so valuable?"

She hesitated.

"It's rather a long story—" she began.

"Never mind how long it is," interrupted Peter. "If you're willing to tell me I'm only too anxious to listen."

For a moment she was silent, and then, apparently making up her mind, she said:

"I think I'd better begin by telling you that I was Harvey Slade's secretary."

Peter looked at her in amazement. This was the last thing he had expected.

"You look surprised," she said with a faint smile. "Yes, I was his secretary, if you could call my position by such a name." She paused a moment, frowned, and then went on: "Harvey Slade was a fence, and I used to smuggle the stuff that came into his possession out of the country."

She watched him to see the effect of this declaration, but although it was something of a shock, Peter managed to return her gaze without blinking.

"Go on," he said quietly.

"I didn't know what I was doing at first," she continued. "In fact, I wasn't sure until six months ago. I first began to get suspicious when he doubled my salary—I was getting quite a big one before—and then as though that were not enough, he began giving me an extra hundred pounds every time I crossed the Channel for him. Knowing his meanness in other things it struck me as strange he should be so generous. It took me some time to find out just how wickedly clever the whole plot was— and then I only found out by accident. The things I used to take across to Antwerp were old books—first editions. There was an old Dutchman—Schweitzer, his name was—who kept a bookstore, and I had to deliver the books to him. He paid me in cash, English money, which I brought back to Slade."

"And do you mean that the stolen stuff was concealed in the books?" exclaimed Peter.

She nodded.

"Yes, but oh, so cleverly! It was jewellery, of course— single stones without their settings—and they were concealed in the bindings where the pages are fixed into the back of the book. You could open the books without discovering anything. Wasn't it clever? You see, the Customs people are not very particular going into the country, and the books were genuine first editions, and some of them were worth quite a lot of money."

"But," said Peter, "when you found out what you were really doing, why didn't you go to the police?"

She looked at him queerly.

"When I've finished, you'll understand," she said. "I told you I found out the real nature of what I was doing by accident. I had been given a book to take over one day which rather interested me. It was full of old woodcuts and instead of packing it up in my little office at once which I usually did, I thought I'd look through it. While I was doing so, I felt something hard in the back and discovered half a dozen large diamonds.

"At first, I was puzzled, and should still have been if Harvey Slade hadn't come in at the moment and caught me. As soon as I saw him, I guessed that there was something wrong about those diamonds. His face was dreadful. For a horrible moment I thought he was going to reach out and strangle me. Then he closed the door and locked it and came over to me. 'So, Miss Inquisitive, you've found the secret out, have you?' he said quietly, and then he told me the truth."

"I still don't see why you didn't go to the police," said Peter, shaking his head. "It was the obvious thing to do."

"I threatened to do so at first," she replied, "but Slade only laughed at me and then showed me just how I stood. He had letters and papers that would have satisfied any judge that I was a party to the business and that I was actually taking my share of the proceeds. Do you see the wicked cleverness of it? That raised salary, the extra hundred pounds every trip I took. He had made me sign a receipt for each one. Would any living jury believe that I was getting a hundred pounds in addition to my salary for taking a parcel of old books across the Channel? And there were letters too. Letters written to Schweitzer explaining who I was and saying that I was perfectly conversant with all matters in which I was dealing. And I had made the journey twenty or thirty times. The Customs people knew me well. Not a living soul would ever have believed for one moment that I was innocent."

"Great Scott! What a ghastly plot!" muttered Peter as he realized that what she said was true. Nobody would believe her. And then an idea occurred to him. "But Slade's dead now," he said. "You're safe enough now."

"Am I?" she answered bitterly. "Don't you see that those letters and receipts are still in existence, and if they get into the hands of the police—"

"By Jove! I never thought of that," said Peter blankly.

"I begged Slade to give them back to me," said Lola. "I offered him most of the money he had given me to let me destroy those letters and receipts and let me go, but he only laughed at me. And he still forced me to go on taking those books across to Amsterdam. Last night he wanted me to go again, and he got angry when I refused and locked me in my office."

"So, you saw nothing of the murder?" said Peter.

"No," she answered. "I only heard him scream. I had arranged to ring up my brother and when I didn't, he came to the house and arrived in time to let me out."

She shuddered.

There was a short silence and then Peter asked suddenly:

"Who is, 'Mr. K.'?"

"He is the man who used to come and see Slade," she answered. "But who he is I don't know. He always wore goggles and a leather motoring helmet, and he never came unless the servants had been sent out. He was there tonight— lurking in the drive—"

"When you went to try and find those letters?" Peter hazarded.

"Yes," she said. "It was a forlorn hope. I had little chance of being able to find them without the pen."

"The pen?" echoed Peter momentarily puzzled, and she explained.

"Somewhere in 'Five Trees' there's a secret safe. I think it's hidden somewhere in the study, but I'm not sure. You see Slade never had a banking account. He kept all his money on the premises."

"And the pen contains the secret of this safe?" asked Peter.
She nodded.

"I think so," she answered. "Once—months ago—I saw Slade scribble something on a piece of paper and put it inside the cap of the pen."

So that was it. Peter understood now why the big man, Ledder, had been so anxious to get the green pen back in his possession. It held the key to a fortune—the accumulated wealth from old Harvey Slade's illegal trading and also those papers incriminating Lola Marsh.

Peter's brows drew down over his eyes thoughtfully. He had offered to help—he wanted very badly to help. How could he?

"You were taking a pretty big risk going to 'Five Trees', weren't you?" he said abruptly. "The servants must be back by now—"

"They came back but they wouldn't stay after they heard what had happened," she said. "They've got a room at the village inn until after the inquest."

"So, there's nobody at 'Five Trees.'" Peter made the statement and at the same time came to his decision. "Miss Marsh, I'm going to have a shot at finding that safe—tonight—and, if the person who pinched that pen from me hasn't got there first, I'll try and bring those letters back to you."

CHAPTER 10

The Man in the Mask

Two o'clock struck on the cracked bell of the little village church and the reverberations were caught up by the wind and whirled away to silence. The solitary constable on guard at the drive gates at 'Five Trees' shivered. With the coming of darkness, the temperature had fallen and although the wind was little more than a breeze, it was cold.

The man stood at the gates and looked down the silent stretch of road for a sight of his relief. He had done his rounds. Lola Marsh, although she hadn't known it, had had a lucky escape, for this policeman had been round at the back when she had come up the drive and, but for her meeting with Mr. K, she would most certainly have encountered him.

Presently as he stood there, he saw his relief come plodding up the road, a lighted cigarette between his lips.

"Alright, Jack?" asked the newcomer as he came up to his companion.

"All quiet on the Western Front," grinned Jack. "Not a darned thing stirring and not a soul about. 'S'nough ter give yer the creeps. Whoever picked this 'ouse for a murder picked a right one." He tucked his rolled-up cape under his arm and prepared to depart. "Well, you've got it for the next eight hours—and you're welcome to it. Goodnight, mate."

He went striding off down the road, little thinking that his casual goodnight was really goodbye, and that he was destined never to see the man who had relieved him alive again.

As his footsteps faded away, a great and somehow ominous silence settled down again over the darkness.

The constable who had remained behind squinted over his shoulder into the shadows of the driveway. All was black and silent. There was a lull in the wind and not even the great trees that flanked the borders rustled. He grunted and threw away his cigarette. Duty was duty and he had to do it, however unpleasant the task.

Switching on his flashlamp, he went quietly up the drive towards the house. As he disappeared, a shadow, black on the blackness of the high hedge on the other side of the roadway, broke away from its shelter and stealing across was swallowed up in the darkness of the drive.

With his heart beating faster than usual, Peter Lake stole cautiously along the grass border towards the dimly-seen bulk of the house. He had had great difficulty in persuading Lola Marsh to let him undertake his mission, but he had succeeded in insisting that the girl should wait for him until he came back. And he had reached 'Five Trees' in time to see the constable at the gates.

It had given him something of a shock, for he had not reckoned on the place being guarded and his first thought had been to give up the venture. And then the thought of going back to the girl and confessing failure after all had urged him on and he had decided to risk it. In any case it was going to be difficult, for he realized now that he was actually on the spot, that even if he found Harvey Slade's hidden safe, it would be next to impossible to open it.

But Peter was an optimist and a great believer in luck. He had read somewhere that a combination safe could be opened by listening for the fall of the tumblers as the dial was turned, and he had brought a stethoscope with him.

Reaching the top of the drive, he waited in the concealment of the shrubbery for the return of the constable and presently he saw his dancing light. The man passed him at barely three yards distance, and two minutes later Peter was creeping in at the dining room window. Without making a sound, he closed the sash behind him and slipped the catch. For some seconds, he stood motionless in the stillness of that house where death in

161

the guise of murder had paid so recent a visit, and then he felt his way out into the hall.

He remembered the position of the study door and crept towards it. It was shut, but he turned the handle and entered the room.

He had provided himself with a torch, over the lens of which he had stuck some black court-plaster with a hole in the centre just sufficiently large to allow a pencil of light to shine through. He fumbled for this now and, switching it on, sent the narrow beam travelling slowly over the room. Not a thing had been moved in that place of death. Only in one way was the room different—and Peter noticed the difference with thankfulness. That sprawling thing by the desk had been removed.

He closed the door and going over to the windows pulled the heavy curtains across so that no chance gleam from his masked torch should warn the constable outside of an unlawful presence within. And then he began his search.

He started with the walls, examining them inch by inch, and every now and again tapping at the panelling with his knuckles. But they yielded nothing. No hollow sound rewarded his diligence. By the time he had completed a circuit of the room, Peter was both puzzled and disappointed. For some reason best known to himself he had expected to find the hidden safe in those panelled walls. If it was in the room at all, it was the natural place one would expect to find it.

But was it in the room and what was more, did it exist? Had the girl allowed her imagination to get the better of her? After all she had no proof. It was only an idea based on the fact that old Harvey Slade hadn't possessed a banking account. She had nothing more tangible to go on than that. And yet, of course, when he came to think of it, she was right.

Dealing in stolen jewellery as he had, Slade must have had some place to keep it. He couldn't leave it lying about the room or trust to the flimsy drawers of a desk. The desk! Perhaps there was something there that would give him the clue he was seeking.

Peter went over to the massive piece of furniture and pulled open a drawer. It was empty. He soon discovered that the rest of the drawers were in a like condition. Of course, he might have expected it. The police had taken all the contents for examination.

He went cold as he thought that those papers incriminating the girl might be among them. But, of course, they hadn't been. If they had, she would have been arrested by now. It suddenly struck him that in any case they must know her identity by now. The servants would have given her name and description to them.

Well, so long as those papers did not come to light, she was all right; but how the devil was he to find them?

He stood in the middle of the room and thought. And then from outside he heard the soft crunch of approaching footsteps. The constable was coming round again on his second circuit of the house.

Peter switched out his torch and waited tensely in the dark for the man to finish his rounds and go back to his lonely vigil by the gate.

The footsteps came on, steady and ponderous. Peter heard him rattle the handle of the back door and pass on. Round the side or the house came the measured tread and then, immediately outside the window, it suddenly stopped.

Peter heard a low exclamation and his heart leaped into his mouth. Why had the man stopped? What had he seen? And then he realized, in a sudden burst of enlightenment. Of course, the curtains!

When the man had been round before, they had been open; now his flashlamp had shown him that they were drawn. He knew that somebody was inside the house; somebody who had no right to be there. Peter felt his hands go sticky as he waited there listening. If he were caught, he would have a hard job to explain his presence.

What should he do?

Wait by the front door and make a dash for it when the constable came in? Wait where he was and get out by the window as soon as the man moved away? Or try to get out by the back?

It depended which way the policeman went when he moved.

He strained his ears, but no sound came now from outside. Guessing that something was wrong the constable was not advertising his movements.

An eternity seemed to pass and still there was silence— complete unbroken silence. Peter felt the sweat break out on his forehead. What was the man doing out there?

At last, he could stand it no longer and, making up his mind, he crept out into the hall. If the constable came that way, he could dash past him in the darkness and, if he came the other way, he would hear him and still make his escape by the front door. He reached the hall and stopped to listen again. This time he heard something—the crunch of a footstep on the gravel. So, the constable was coming that way, was he? Pressing himself against the wall, he waited; his muscles tense. There came the click of metal against metal warning him that a key was turning in the lock. He braced himself for the rush as a breath of cool air fanned his heated face, and then, with a sudden blaze, the hall lights came on.

Peter's breath left his lungs in a gasp of sheer astonishment, for instead of the constable, there stood on the threshold a tall, gaunt figure, clad entirely in black, whose malevolent eyes stared at him menacingly through the slits in the mask that concealed his face!

CHAPTER 11

Danger!

The man in the mask stood motionless, one gloved hand on the electric light switches, the other gripped round the butt of a wicked-looking automatic, and the astonished Peter gave a little shiver as he looked at this unexpected apparition, for the half-glimpsed eyes were evilly malignant.

"Well," snarled a harsh voice. "What are you doing here?"

There was a curious intensity about that voice. It was low and oddly distinct, with a quality of hard sibilance about it that was as penetrating as a bullet.

Peter stared at the masked face and kept silent. Without shifting his eyes from Peter's face, the masked man advanced a couple of paces, and closed the door.

"You, I suppose, are Dr. Lake?" he said thoughtfully.

"Your supposition is right," replied Peter, recovering a little from his first shock of surprise. "May I ask who you are?"

"You may ask," answered the other, "but I shan't answer. It is no concern of yours who I am."

"I see," said Peter pleasantly, but his eyes narrowed. "Well, I should put away that gun if 1 were you and clear out. Perhaps you don't know it, but there's a constable outside, and I don't think it will be very long before he's inside."

The masked man shrugged his shoulders.

"That is where you are wrong," he retorted. "There was a constable outside. I have been watching him for quite a while. I can assure you, however, that he will not interfere."

Peter went suddenly cold.

"You mean—" he cried hoarsely.

"I mean," said the other quickly, "that he is no longer in a position to take any further interest in the proceedings. It is quite remarkable how chloroform affects people like that." His voice changed and became tense and menacing. "Now, Dr. Lake, without wasting further time, where is that pen?"

Peter frowned.   So here was another one after the pen.

"I haven't the least idea," he replied steadily.

"You haven't the least idea?" repeated the black-clad figure softly. "Then what are you doing here?"

Peter tried to think of a convincing answer to this question, failed and said nothing.

"Come, come, Dr. Lake," snapped the masked man impatiently. "If you have no knowledge of the green pen—if you do not know of its significance—why are you in this house at so late an hour?"

"That is my business," said Peter.

"You'll find that it's mine also," snarled the other. "Stop being a fool and give me that pen."

"I haven't got the pen," said Peter, and wondered how many times during the past forty-eight hours he had made the same remark.

"But you know what it contained—you found the paper in the cap?" insisted the man in the mask.

"Supposing I did," snapped Peter angrily. "What about it?"

The eyes regarding him through the silken slits glittered evilly.

"This about it," said the voice threateningly, and the tall figure moved forward until the muzzle of the automatic was barely three inches from Peter's stomach. "If you know what that pen contained you will tell—now—unless you want to go the same way as—the policeman."

The gloved forefinger moved, compressing slightly on the trigger, and Peter thought rapidly.

"You daren't shoot," he said, keeping his voice steady with a supreme effort. "Not in your own interests—for if you kill me, I certainly shan't be able to tell you anything about the pen."

There was a tense silence during which Peter felt the perspiration trickle down his forehead, and then the masked man took a step backwards.

"There is something in what you say," he muttered, and then, before Peter could fully appreciate the relief that came to him: "I will try other methods, perhaps less pleasant."

Without removing his gaze from Peter, he whistled—a soft, low whistle. There was a moment's pause and then the door, which he had closed, opened and a small man came in.

"Bilter," said the man in black, "you have the chloro-form—"

He left the sentence unfinished, nodding his head towards Peter. The little wizened man shot a quick glance round and took from his pocket a bottle and a pad.

Peter clenched his fists.

"Look here—" he began angrily, but the masked man stopped him with a peremptory gesture.

"You keep quiet," he snarled, "otherwise this gun may go off with unpleasant consequences. Now, Bilter."

Bilter advanced with a hideous grin distorting his ugly pockmarked face and, as he came, he uncorked the bottle and soaked the pad of cotton wool he held with its contents. Peter smelt the sickly odour, like rotten apples, and the scent made him throw caution to the winds.

"You dirty little rat!" he cried. "You can keep that stuff away from me!"

He sprang forward and launched himself at the cowering Bilter. The man collapsed under Peter's onslaught and they fell to the floor a struggling mass, with Peter uppermost. The masked man gave an exclamation of anger and stepped forward. Gripping his pistol by the barrel, he raised it, and waiting his opportunity brought it down with his force on the back of Peter's skull. Peter gave a little coughing grunt and rolled over at his feet, unconscious.

167

*   *   *   *

Lola Marsh sat on the settee in the tiny consulting room and watched the minute hand of her wristwatch moving slowly round. Over and over again she blamed herself for having let Peter go and, as the time went on, she found it increasingly difficult to master her growing fear.

A hundred visions of what might be happening at that dark and deserted house to which he had gone so light heartedly flickered before her imagination and more than once she rose with the intention of going there herself and finding out what was actually occurring. The goggled man might have gone back after his unsuccessful attempt to capture her. The goggled man—the killer of Harvey Slade—Mr. K.—

Her fear grew until it was a monster choking her. If only she had somebody there with her to whom she could talk! She looked at the telephone with some vague idea of ringing her brother up, but he would be in bed and asleep. Apart from which he had no idea that she had started on her mad visit to the old house—was under the impression that she had gone to bed.

She got up and began walking the room restlessly. Had Peter been successful? Had he found the hidden safe, and would she experience on his return the relief of knowing that those papers were no longer a source of danger?

For some reason or other she felt a vague foreboding—a subconscious warning of impending peril. It made her start at every sound—the creaking of a floorboard; the breeze brushing a branch across the window; the hundred-and-one night noises that in the country seem to spring up like uneasy ghosts in the darkness.

She ought never to have let him go. She knew the danger more than he—knew the stake for which these people were playing—knew just how desperate they were. If anything happened to Peter she would feel like a murderess.

She stopped suddenly in her mechanical pacing to and fro—and stopped and stood rigid. Was that the click of the gate? She listened.

Yes, she could hear footsteps coming up the gravel path leading to the front door. A wave of relief passed over her as she realized that her fears had been groundless. Here was Peter, and whether he had been successful or not she didn't care. He was back, and that was all that mattered.

She heard the key in the lock and the door open and, unable to curb her impatience, went into the little hall.

"I'm so glad," she began, and stopped, the words frozen on her lips.

Instead of Peter, she could see in the dim shadows the figures of two men, and they were carrying the limp body of a third between them! She heard a snarling oath as the taller of the two dropped his burden and sprang at her, caught a momentary glimpse of a masked face close to her own and then everything was gone—wiped out by unconsciousness!

CHAPTER 12

The Ordeal

Peter Lake slid back to consciousness slowly and to the accompaniment of an ever-increasing pain in his head. To ease this, he tried to put up his hand to his throbbing temples and found that he could not. He found also that he could not move any of his other limbs either and opened his eyes. At first, he could see nothing for the light made his head swim; but gradually this passed off and to his astonishment he saw that he was lying on the settee in his own consulting room. How had he got there? And why couldn't he use his arms and legs?

And then he heard the dim murmur of voices and, raising his head, he saw that besides himself there were two other people in the room—a tall gaunt man, whose face was hidden behind a square of black silk, and a little wizened pockmarked fellow. Memory came flooding back and as it did, so he saw the fourth occupant of the room, and a cry escaped his lips.

Bound to a chair so securely that she could not move hand or foot and with a gag tied round her mouth, was Lola Marsh. Her wide violet-blue eyes were fixed on his with an expression in which fear and relief were curiously mingled.

At his cry the tall man who had been talking to his companion in low tones swung round and corning over to the settee, stood looking down at him.

"Got your senses back, have you?" he said, nodding. "Well, that's good. Now we can talk!"

"Don't talk too much, guv'nor," interrupted Bilter anxiously. "We 'aven't got all the time in the world."

"You mind your own business!" snarled Paul Andronsky. "I'm looking after this job."

Bilter shrugged his narrow shoulders.

"Alright," he protested. "I'm only tellin' yer that the night doesn't last for ever, and we want ter get done and away before it gets light."

"We'll do that—you needn't worry," retorted the masked man. "Now, Dr. Lake, I hope you are going to be sensible and save me all further trouble and yourself a great deal of—shall we say inconvenience?"

Peter looked up at him, and his lips compressed.

"I don't know what you're talking about," he said, weakly, "but I warn you that you'd better release that girl at once, or—"

"Or what?" broke in Andronsky with a sneer. "Believe me your threats do not frighten me in the least. I need hardly remind you that you are not in a position to dictate to me. Indeed, the shoe is on the other foot. However, the release of Miss Marsh is entirely in your hands. If you are sensible, she will not be harmed in any way."

"What do you want?" asked Peter, knowing full well but trying to gain time while he forced his brain to cope with the situation.

"I want the green pen which that fool, Ledder, dropped in the drive at 'Five Trees' and which you picked up," said the masked man. "Or, alternatively, I want to know what was in it."

"I haven't got the pen," said Peter, "and neither do I know what was in it."

The eyes behind the black silk regarded him suspiciously.

"Did you give the pen to Ledder then?" asked Andronsky.

"I did not," replied Peter, "for the simple reason that it wasn't in my possession."

"I don't believe you!" snarled the masked man. "If you didn't give it to Ledder, it's still in your possession."

"You are at liberty to search the whole house," retorted Peter, "and if you can find it, you're cleverer than I am."

Paul Andronsky laughed and shook his head.

171

"I daresay, my friend," he answered softly, "but you are not getting me to waste my time like that. I should prefer you to tell me exactly where that pen is."

"I'm not good at performing miracles," said Peter, "and it would be a miracle if I could tell you where the pen is."

Andronsky leaned down over the settee until Peter could feel his hot breath fanning his cheek.

"So, you insist on sticking to that story, do you?" he grated harshly. "You think you can fool me and get away with it? I warn you, my friend, that you had better change your mind."

"Look here!" said Peter, staring up at the other steadily. "Suppose we cut out all this melodramatic rubbish! Once and for all I haven't got the pen! I don't know where it is, and I don't know what is in it! Have you got that clear?"

"You put up a very good bluff, Dr. Lake," said Andronsky, "and it might have the effect of fooling some people, but it doesn't go with me. I have no wish to resort to strong methods, but unless you are willing to be sensible, I'm afraid I shall have to. For the last time, will you tell me what you have done with that pen?"

"I've said all I've got to say," snapped Peter angrily, "and I'm not going to keep up this cross talk any longer!"

Paul Andronsky straightened up to his full height.

"I'm afraid you are labouring under a delusion," he said, and his voice was vibrant with suppressed anger. "You will say a great deal more before I've finished with you and the young lady!"

He turned as he spoke the last words and looked at the girl.

For the first time, Peter felt a twinge of alarm.

"You can leave Miss Marsh out of it," he said hastily. "She's got nothing to do with it!"

The man in the mask gave a low malignant chuckle.

"That is another delusion of yours, Dr. Lake," he sneered. "You seem to be full of them. Miss Marsh has everything to do with it—as you will see in a few seconds."

"What do you mean?" demanded Peter.

"If you continue in your pig-headed refusal to divulge what you have done with the pen," said Paul Andronsky, and there was cold ferocity in his emotionless voice, "I shall have to take steps to make you! That is where Miss Marsh will be of the greatest assistance."

The blood receded from Peter's face leaving it white and strained. There was no mistaking the threat that lay behind the man's words.

Andronsky saw by his expression that he understood his meaning and laughed again—a hard sound without any vestige of mirth.

"I see that you understand," he said softly. "Perhaps, without going to—er—such lengths, you will do what I ask?"

The momentary feeling of cold fear left Peter and was replaced by a flaming anger against this sneering chuckling devil, who was suggesting unnameable things.

"You infernal scoundrel!" he roared, wrenching furiously at the cords which bound his wrists. "If you touch a hair of that girl's head, I'll—"

"You'll do what?" broke in Andronsky harshly. "What will you do, Dr. Lake? Please tell me. It would interest me." And then suddenly changing his tone: "You fool! What can you do? Why not stop all these cheap heroics and be sensible!"

"I've already told you," panted Peter, "that even if my life depended on it I couldn't tell you what you want to know!"

"And I have said that I don't believe you," snarled the masked man. "Apart from which it is not your life that is in any danger."

He stopped and turning, looked at the terrified girl.

"Have you noticed," he went on, "what really beautiful hands Miss Marsh has? So white and well-kept and with such long tapering fingers. What a pity it would be if anything should happen to spoil them!"

He paused and, with Peter's eyes riveted on him, walked over to a small glass-fronted cabinet in the corner.

"Your profession will save me a great deal of trouble, Dr. Lake," he murmured, tapping the glass door with a gloved finger. "Everything I require is here to my hand."

Peter watched frozen with horror. He knew only too well what that cabinet contained—the rows of shining, razor-sharp surgical instruments that he so conscientiously kept clean, but up to now had had no occasion to use.

"With one of these slender knives," said Andronsky, "it will be child's play to remove the fingers from Miss Marsh's beautiful right hand—one by one—"

"You fiend!" burst out Peter through lips that were white and bloodless. "You can't do it!"

Paul Andronsky shrugged his shoulders and, pulling open the cabinet, selected a scalpel which he balanced in one hand.

"I can—and I will—do just that," he said, "unless you do what I ask. I am not a skilled surgeon, and I don't expect to perform the—er—operation so well as you would, for inst-ance. There will, no doubt, be considerable pain, and loss of blood—"

"By heaven!" shouted Peter, "If I was only free—"

"If the earth was made of bread and cheese," scoffed Andronsky. "You are making a great fuss, Dr. Lake—a foolish fuss, for what I propose doing is in your power to prevent!"

Peter suppressed a groan. That was just it, it was not in his power to prevent this outrage, but the fiend in the mask would never believe it.

"Stop!" he cried hoarsely, as Andronsky went over to the girl with the knife in his hand. "Stop! Listen to me! Don't you

174

realize that I would give up a thousand green pens to stop Miss Marsh from being harmed?"

"I only ask you to give up one," interrupted the masked man. "Give me that or tell where it is, and I'll go at once."

"But I can't," said Peter desperately. "I keep telling you I can't! Don't you understand plain English?"

"Then I'm afraid we shall have to continue the comedy," snapped Andronsky. "I can't afford to waste any further time." He bent over the white-faced girl and picked up her slender right hand. She shrank away and Peter heard, in spite of the gag, her strangled cry of terror.

"For the love of heaven don't do it," cried Peter, half-crazy at his helplessness.

Andronsky took no notice, and the glittering knife touched the girl's first finger.

"I hate spoiling anything so beautiful," he said softly. But you leave me no alternative."

The keen blade pressed against the soft flesh, and a little line of crimson showed up with startling clearness. Lola Marsh gave a choking cry, and then Bilter, who had been a fascinated and silent spectator hitherto, sprang forward and caught her as she swayed.

"Stop!" cried Peter, the perspiration standing out in great beads on his forehead. "Stop, I'll tell you what you want to know."

Andronsky straightened up and his eyes glittered.

"I thought you would," he said, with a note of triumph in his voice. "Come, quickly! Tell me where it is?"

Peter collected his scattered wits and lied.

"You'll find the pen in my bedroom," he said. "In the chimney. I put it—"

He broke off with a gasp of astonishment as a strange high-pitched voice said:

"Thank you, Dr. Lake! That information is going to be very useful!"

Andronsky gave a hoarse cry and dropped the knife, staring beyond Peter's head at something on the other side of the room. With an effort Peter twisted round and saw, framed in the open doorway, his head encased in a leather helmet and the upper part of his face concealed by a pair of mica goggles, the sinister figure of Mr. K.!

CHAPTER 13

The End of Andronsky

Superintendent Robert Budd flung the black stub of a cigar into the fireplace, shifted his huge bulk until he was more comfortably settled in the big armchair, carefully arranged a cushion behind his head and sighed. The accommodation which he had secured at the only inn that Higher Wicklow boasted was extremely comfortable.

With his large body at rest in one chair and his feet supported on a second chair, the Rosebud pondered on the whole tricky problem.

A telephone message, following his substantial dinner, had given him all the information he wanted to know regarding Ledder. The man had never come in direct contact with the police, neither was he known in 'Records', but he had apparently been the associate and friend of people less fortunate in this respect than himself.

Paul Andronsky, with whom he had been seen on several occasions, was a well-known crook who had served two sentences for fraud, from the last of which he had only just been released. This information gave Mr. Budd food for much thought, for he remembered that the first person to suffer from the elusive Mr. K.'s attentions had been Lew Andronsky, the brother of this recently released convict.

He lit another long, black, evil-smelling cigar and smoked with closed eyes. Yes, undoubtedly, the case was tricky. There were so many people in it.

Mr. Budd opened his eyes, blew a large cloud of rank smoke from his lips, watched it disperse, and closed his eyes again. The girl. He had learned quite a lot about her from the servants, and there was still quite a lot that he wanted to know. For one thing, he was still very anxious to know where she was

177

to be found. Neither the old man nor the old woman could tell him where she lived. Yes, there was quite a lot of mystery surrounding the girl that wanted clearing up.

Mr. Budd relapsed into such a state of intense mental concentration that anybody seeing him at that moment would have been convinced that he had fallen asleep.

The whole secret lay in that pen—and Mr. K., he finally decided.

The cone of ash on his cigar grew longer and longer and presently dropped on to his waistcoat. But he might have been dead for all the notice he took, and it was not until the glowing end had reached his fingers that he started to wakefulness, and then he became surprisingly wakeful indeed.

The inn had long since closed and the inmates were in bed and asleep—even Mr. Budd himself was a little surprised when he saw the time—but it did not prevent him from putting his suddenly conceived plan into execution.

It has been said by his confreres at Scotland Yard that Superintendent Robert Budd was never known to be fully awake. This gross slander would have been refuted if any of them could have seen him during the following half-hour, for in spite of the lateness of the hour, he swiftly donned hat and coat and, creeping down the stairs, let himself silently out into the cold darkness of the night. A sharp glance he gave to right and left, and then set off briskly along the deserted road...

*   *   *   *

"So, you weren't wise enough to take my advice, Andronsky, eh?" said the high-pitched voice. "I told you to keep out of this!"

"I don't take orders from anybody!" Paul Andronsky crouched back against the wall glaring hate at the newcomer through the slits in his mask.

"The time is coming very shortly when you won't be able to take orders from anybody—except the devil," answered Mr. K. gently and waved the automatic which he held in his hand. "In the meanwhile, I'm afraid I shall have to take steps to ensure that you do not make a nuisance of yourself."

He turned his head towards the shivering and terrified Bilter, and the light glinting on the mica eyepieces of his goggles gave him a peculiarly eerie inhuman appearance.

"You there," he said harshly, "pull down that curtain from the window, tear it in strips, and tie up our friend here."

He nodded towards Andronsky. Bilter hesitated, torn between his fear of Andronsky and his terror of Mr. K.

"Come on," grated the latter sharply. "Do as you're told, otherwise I shall regret being so lenient." The muzzle of the automatic moved menacingly and with a little gasp of abject terror Bilter hastened to obey.

Mr. K. watched him in silence.

"That's better," he said when Andronsky's wrists and ankles had been securely bound and he had examined the knots. "Now come here."

Bilter approached, licking his dry lips apprehensively.

"Give me the rest of that curtain stuff," said the goggled man. "Now turn round and cross your wrists behind your back."

Bilter did as he was told, and in a few seconds had been trussed up as securely as his companion.

Mr. K pocketed his pistol and stood surveying his handiwork with satisfaction.

"That's much better," he remarked.

"What are you going to do with us?" snarled Andronsky, and there was a slight shake in his voice that was not due to anger.

"At the present moment you're alright as you are," replied Mr. K. "What I may do with you later I haven't yet decided."

179

He looked at Peter. "I am going to collect that pen first. You say it's in the chimney in your bedroom, Dr. Lake? If you will excuse me, I will go and get it."

He turned abruptly before Peter could reply and went out into the darkness of the hall. A silence followed his exit. What, thought Peter, was going to happen when he discovered that there was no pen in the chimney?

He looked at Andronsky. The masked man was struggling with the bonds at his wrists and breathing heavily as a result of his exertions. The girl was still slumped in the chair unconscious, a thin trickle of blood running down her fingers. Bilter lay motionless on the floor, his little beady eyes staring at the open door. Peter heard Mr. K. ascending the stairs and presently moving about the room overhead.

An eternity seemed to pass. A whole lifetime crowded into the space of a minute. There was no sound from upstairs and Peter guessed that Mr. K. was searching in the chimney for the pen that wasn't there.

A sound from the direction of Andronsky made him look over quickly and, with a start of surprise, he saw that the masked man had succeeded in freeing his hands. Either Bilter had made a bad job of the tying or the curtain strips had stretched.

Andronsky bent down and tore at the knots at his ankles, a moment later he was free. With a quick glance upwards, he went over to the prostrate Bilter and began tugging at the bindings round his wrists. Peter felt his breath coming a little faster. The approach of the crisis was at hand and what the climax would be it was impossible to guess. Mr. K. would be returning shortly from his useless quest and then—what would happen?

The sound of footsteps from above became audible once more. They were crossing the floor, quickly, hastily. Mr. K. had

180

examined the chimney and found—nothing. Now he was coming to demand an explanation.

Andronsky heard the steps and stopped in his endeavours to free his companion. With a quick spring, he was across the room and, stooping, picked up the knife which had fallen from his hand at the appearance of the goggled man. Grasping it like a dagger, he tiptoed over to the open doorway, and stood pressed up against the wall at the side of the door.

The footsteps of Mr. K. began to descend the stairs and Peter saw Andronsky grow rigid.

A dim figure loomed in the doorway, and he opened his mouth to cry out. But even as the cry left his lips, Andronsky sprang forward and struck with all his force at the breast of the man crossing the threshold. There was a metallic snap and a snarled oath, and then Andronsky staggered back, glaring at the broken knife in his hand.

"You fool!" snarled Mr. K. "Do you think you could get me like that? I'm wearing a bullet proof waistcoat."

He whipped out his automatic from his pocket and sent three shots tearing through the body of the crouching man before him. Andronsky gave a choking cough, clawed at the air, and pitched forward on his face.

CHAPTER 14

Fire!

Taking no notice of Peter's horrified exclamation, Mr. K. walked over to the sprawling body of his victim and spurned it contemptuously with his foot. When he had made quite certain that Andronsky was dead, he pocketed the still-smoking automatic and came over to the settee.

"Dr. Lake," he said calmly as though nothing had happened, "there is no pen in the chimney. Will you kindly give me an explanation?"

With an effort Peter dragged his eyes away from that huddled body and the ever-widening pool that was spreading over the shabby carpet and looked up at the goggled man.

"I lied to Andronsky," he said. "He wouldn't believe me when I said I hadn't got the pen and didn't know where it was, and so I lied—to stop him torturing Miss Marsh."

He saw the lips compress and guessed that Mr. K. was frowning.

"And is it true that you don't know the whereabouts of the pen?" asked Mr. K. after a slight pause.

"Perfectly true," said Peter. "If I had I should have told Andronsky before he went to the lengths he did."

There was a silence. The goggled man appeared to be thinking deeply.

"Extraordinary," he muttered presently. "Where the devil can it be? You haven't got it; the girl hasn't got it. Ledder didn't get it, and Andronsky obviously didn't get it. Where can it be?"

"I haven't the least idea," said Peter, answering his spoken thoughts. "Somebody must have taken it from me while I lay unconscious in that house."

"There was nobody to take it," said Mr. K. "Only the people I have mentioned knew of its significance." He broke off suddenly, and Peter saw that he was listening intently.

Peter listened too, but at first, he could hear nothing, and then from outside came the sound of footsteps on gravel. They stopped, came on again, and stopped once more—uncertain hesitating footsteps. Mr. K. went over to the door and stood; his head inclined forward into the darkness of the little hall.

Rat-tat, rat-tat. Somebody was knocking softly at the front door. Peter's heart bounded with sudden hope. There was only one person who would be likely to call at that hour and that was Mr. Budd. And yet the step had not sounded like his, neither was the knock incisive enough. He heard the goggled man utter a soft curse and saw him move out into the hall and become lost in the blackness. There was a pause, and then the knocking on the front door was repeated, this time a little louder. There was the click of a lock, and then a voice said:

"Can I see Dr. Lake?"

It was followed by a startled cry and the heavy slam of the front door shutting. Before the wondering Peter had time to conjecture what had happened, Mr. K. came back, dragging with him the stooping figure of an elderly man whose lined face was twisted into an expression of sheer terror.

"Now then, what do you want to see Dr. Lake for?" snarled Mr. K. flinging his captive away from him so that he staggered and fell back against the wall.

With a thrill of intense surprise Peter saw that the newcomer was Harvey Slade's old servant. The man was in the last stages of fear. His eyes bulged from his head and his jaws hung loosely. Peter, who had never met the man to speak to before in his life, wondered what on earth had brought him there.

"Now then, out with it!" snapped Mr. K. catching the terrified old man by the arm and shaking him roughly. "What did you come to see Dr. Lake for?"

The other made an unintelligible sound in his throat.

"Answer me!" cried Mr. K. shaking him again and then, as the old man opened his mouth, he gave a loud exultant exclamation, and tearing back his coat, snatched from his waistcoat pocket something that glinted greenly in the electric light.

Peter echoed his cry in his astonishment, for the thing he held in his hand was the green fountain pen that had belonged to Harvey Slade!

"How did you get this?" hissed Mr. K.

The old man swallowed hard and crouched farther back against the wall.

"I—I took it from Dr. Lake's pocket after 'e was knocked out up at the 'ouse," he stammered almost inaudibly. "I didn't mean no 'arm—"

"So, you were there that night, were you?" broke in the goggled man. The other nodded feebly.

"Yes, I come back," he said. "I wondered why the guv'nor used to send me and the missus away at times, and I thought I'd come back and find out.

"Just as I got back, I saw Dr. Lake having a fight with a big chap in the drive and I saw 'im pick up that pen. I knew it contained the secret of the guv'nor's safe, but I 'adn't no idea of taking it then. It was only arter I got up to the 'ouse and saw 'e'd been killed and that Dr. Lake 'ad been 'it on the 'ead that I thought p'r'haps if I took it, I might be able ter open the safe and get a few pickings.

"Then I saw that Dr. Lake was recovering and I got scared and cleared off. Afterwards when all the fuss was on and the perlice was 'anging about, I didn't like to say anything about it, but the missus thought I didn't ought ter keep it, and p'r'aps if I brought it back to Dr. Lake and explained 'e'd save me from gettin' inter trouble—" His voice trailed away incoherently.

"So that was it, was it?" muttered Mr. K. "Well, you couldn't have chosen a better time so far as I'm concerned, though I doubt whether it will be so from your point of view."

He unscrewed the cap of the pen and carefully extracted a small roll of paper. Spreading it out, he glanced at it quickly and then put it in his pocket.

"I'll make you a present of this," he said, tossing the pen on to the settee. "I've got all I want."

He seized the old man by the arm and dragged him away from the wall and then, with a strip of curtain that was left over, securely bound his wrists and ankles.

"Now you're all comfy," he said with a quick glance round.

"Yer ain't going ter leave me like this," whined Bilter, "fer the perlice ter find? Don't do that guv'nor. You've got what you wanted, and I ain't done nothin' ter 'arm yer. Let me go—"

"The police won't find you, I promise that," said Mr. K. "There will, in fact, be nothing for them to find."

His words made Peter go suddenly cold. What further devilry had the man planned? A second later he had discovered and was appalled, for Mr. K. without another word went swiftly over to the window, tore down the remaining curtain and draped it over Peter's desk. A pile of newspapers on a corner table he fetched over and scattered on top of the curtain and then, from his pocket, he produced a petrol lighter, snapped it open and applied the flame to the flimsy curtain stuff. It caught at once and a long yellow tongue of fire engulfed the desk, licking hungrily at the dry woodwork.

Mr. K. turned quickly.

"Goodbye," he said, and walked to the door. "The dawn is always a little chilly, but I think you will be warm enough!"

* * * *

185

Mr. Robert Budd plodded along the deserted country road; his mind fully occupied in turning over the idea that had come to him. It was a long way from the inn to 'Five Trees' and the Rosebud hated exercise of any sort, but he went on, his fat legs covering the ground at a surprising speed.

He reached the dark forbidding entrance to the drive and paused, looking about him for the man on guard. But there was no sign of him. The winding tree-bordered stretch of moss-covered gravel faded into the blackness, empty and devoid of life.

Mr. Budd grunted. The constable, of course, was on his rounds somewhere up by the house. The stout superintendent entered the gates and began to walk up the avenue. He came in sight of the house—dark, gloomy and uninviting and paused again. Still no sign of the constable.

He moved on again towards the house and rounded the angle of the side wall. Here the overshadowing trees formed a patch of dense blackness and Mr. Budd had to pick his way carefully. He had not gone more than eight yards when his foot caught in something, and he stumbled and nearly fell. The muttered curse which had risen to his lips died as his hand, which he had flung out to save himself, came in contact with—flesh!

He sat back on his haunches and fumbled in his pocket for a box of matches, his heart beating fast. The first match blew out, but the second he shielded with his palm, and in its feeble glimmer he saw the motionless form and white, upturned face of the constable. He was stone dead and across his mouth still rested the chloroform-soaked pad of cottonwool that had killed him.

The Rosebud grunted and got to his feet as the match burned to his fingers and went out. He was by no means a coward, but he gave a quick and uneasy glance behind him as he stood in the darkness. Was the murderer of the constable still lurking somewhere near the house? Watching him, perhaps, from the concealment of that sweeping belt of shrubbery.

The hair stirred slightly on his neck and then he gave himself a shake. This would never do. He was giving way to nerves. A man had been killed in the execution of his duty and it was his duty to pull in the killer.

Leaving the body where he had found it, he walked round the house, keeping as sharp a lookout as he could. But there was no sight or sound of any other living presence.

He decided to go and set off down the drive at a run.

He was panting heavily from his unusual exertion as he came up the village High Street, and then at the far end he saw a glow of light—an ominous red glow that cast a ruddy glare on the roadway. Dark figures were moving in the light of the flames and, as he breathlessly rounded the bend of the road and came in sight of the blazing house, the last of his breath left him in a gasp of surprise. The house that was burning so furiously was Dr. Lake's!

*   *   *   *

The wind whispered softly high up in the tree-tops round 'Five Trees,' and blew gently in cool, caressing gusts over the white face of the dead man who lay under the shadow of those gloomy walls, staring sightlessly into the black vault of the sky. It blew gently in at the half-open window of the dining room and stirred the curtains as though unseen fingers were pulling them inside and sent little breaths through the open door into the dark hall, but the closed door of the study checked it.

Behind that closed door, in the big room where Harvey Slade had lived and worked and died, the man who had killed him sent the dancing light of a torch leaping over the dim apartment. He was breathing quickly with excitement as he advanced to the huge desk that occupied the centre of the room

187

and, standing beside it, consulted the slip of paper in his hand. He had pushed his goggles up on to his forehead, and his eyes, as he scanned the written lines, were full of greed. Here, close at hand, was the fortune that old Slade had tried to do him out of. Half of it at least was his by right, for it had been his brain that had put it into Slade's possession. Fifty-fifty had been the arrangement, and he had been content with that. But Slade hadn't. Slade had wanted the lot, and more! Well, he was dead, and now he would get nothing.

He swung the torch round and directed its light on to one of the massive carved legs of the desk. The third acorn—that was it! He felt along the wood and pressed. There was a faint click as a piece of the carving sank beneath his thumb. And that was all—nothing else happened. He scowled and looked at the slip of paper again. Yes, he had followed the directions, but—

He flashed the torch around him and then he saw what he had not noticed before. A small block of the parquet flooring near the desk had risen on end. He went over eagerly and, directing his light into the cavity, saw a small, polished steel knob projecting. Kneeling down, he put in his hand and grasping the knob, he pulled...

CHAPTER 15

Raining Money

Peter watched the fire rapidly gaining ground with a feeling of helpless despair. So this was the end. In less than an hour, unless somebody came to their rescue, they would be burned up in that holocaust—black, charred, unrecognizable.

Peter racked his brains to find some way out of this deathtrap. The desk was blazing furiously, and the carpet near where it stood had started to smoulder. It was this that gave him his idea. With a desperate effort he rolled himself off the settee, falling with a thud that shook the room and sent a shower of sparks flying up from the burning wood. With difficulty he rolled himself over towards the blazing mass where the fire had started and then, gritting his teeth, he thrust his bound wrist into the flame.

The pain was excruciating, and he had to bite his tongue to prevent the cry which rose in his throat escaping. The sweat poured down his forehead, but he achieved his object. In a little while he felt his bonds give, and then as he jerked his wrists apart, they snapped.

His hands and wrists were scorched and blistered, but he was free. With frantic haste he untied his ankles and staggered to his feet. An instant later he was bending over Lola and feverishly tugging at the knots that bound her.

"You get outside and wait for me," he said chokingly as the smoke caught at his throat and set him coughing. She hesitated, but he helped her to her feet and pushed her towards the door.

"Go quickly," he said. "I'll follow you in a second."

She obeyed and going over to Bilter he stooped and set the little crook free. The strain of the last few seconds had been too much for the man. He had fainted. Peter picked him up, carried him across the hall to the front door and slung him out into the garden. Then he went back for the old servant. By the time he had released him the whole room was blazing furiously, and even as he and the old man reached the door, he heard a crash as the ceiling in one corner fell.

Lola Marsh was waiting by the front door, and as they came into the cool air, with eyes smarting and streaming from the effects of the smoke, she grasped his arm.

Blindly she led him down the little path, the old servant stumbling along behind them, through the gate and out into the roadway, which was lit almost to the brightness of day by the lurid, rapidly spreading flames from the burning house.

As Peter paused and wiped his streaming forehead with the back of his hand, he heard the irregular thudding of approaching footsteps. Turning he saw a man running jerkily towards them—a big man who was panting heavily—and as he came into the light Peter recognized him.

"Mr. Budd!" he gasped, and the runner stopped.

"What's been happening here?" panted the Rosebud with difficulty; and as briefly as he could Peter told him.

"Then he's gone to the house—'Five Trees'," snapped the stout inspector. "If we're quick we can catch him—wait there!" He was off again, leaving Peter standing in the roadway with Lola Marsh and the terrified servant.

The girl touched him on the arm and, looking down into her upturned face, Peter saw that it was troubled.

"If—if the police catch Mr. K. and open that safe, she whispered, "they'll find those papers."

"I'm afraid they will," broke in Peter, "and I don't see how we are going to prevent it. The only thing you can do is tell Budd the truth. He seems a decent sort."

"He'll never believe my story," she said, shaking her head. "But I suppose it's the only thing to do now."

The fire had at last attracted the attention of the sleeping villagers, and excited voices heralded the appearance of partially dressed members of the community.

They came running towards the spot and surrounded the little group, gesticulating violently, and all speaking at once. Before Peter could answer any of their questions, however, the sound of a motor-horn sent them scattering, and an open Ford drew up beside Peter with a shrill squeaking of brakes.

"Jump in," called the voice of the Rosebud from the back, "both of you and bring the old man with you."

Peter bundled the dazed old man in with Mr. Budd and his companion, whom he recognized as Inspector Bullot. He had barely had time to scramble in himself before the car started with a jerk and shot off up the High Street. Fifty yards away from the drive entrance to 'Five Trees,' the superintendent stopped it.

"We don't want to let him know we've come," he said as he got out. "You come with us, Dr. Lake. Miss Marsh can stop here with Sergeant Dobson."

Lola opened her lips to protest, thought better of it and remained silent, but Peter caught her appealing glance as he followed Bullot and the Rosebud, and gave her a nod of encouragement.

The drive was black and silent as they entered it, and picking their way noiselessly on the grassy border, made towards the house. The dark bulk of the building loomed up evil and sinister against the faint grey that streaked the eastern sky. Suddenly Mr. Budd uttered a hissing warning and Peter felt his arm gripped.

"He's there!" said the stout man and there was a tinge or excitement in his voice and Peter saw a momentary flash from one or the windows.

Cautiously they crept forward.

191

"If possible," whispered Mr. Budd, "we want to take him by surprise."

But it was he who got the surprise, for the end of his sentence was drowned in a shattering explosion that shook the earth beneath their feet and came echoing back from the surrounding hills. The dark bulk of the house was split by a gigantic sheet of white-hot flame and before their eyes they saw the walls crumble.

"My God!" cried Peter. "What's happened?"

The Rosebud, without answering began to run towards the ruin that had been 'Five Trees' and then he stopped, sheltering beneath the trees that lined the drive, for the air suddenly became filled with falling debris. It fell around them thickly, striking the ground with dull thuds and pattering on the leaves above them like rain. Something fluttered into Peter's face and he grabbed it—an oblong white object that cracked in his fingers. In the darkness he caught sight of other dim white shapes that fluttered round him like falling leaves.

The feel of the thing he held brought an exclamation of amazement to his lips.

"Have you got a light?" he asked hoarsely, and Bullot produced a torch and flashed it on.

Peter gave one glance at the object in his hand in the white beam and turned to Mr. Budd.

"Gosh! Look at this!" he exclaimed. "And there's more of them—all round us."

Mr. Budd's large face discarded its habitual half-sleepy, wholly-bored expression.

"Well, I never!" he breathed in astonishment. "It's raining money!" Peter was holding a Bank of England note for a hundred pounds!

*   *   *   *

The explosion had destroyed the greater part of the house and with it the man known as Mr. K. Certain portions of a human body were found among the ruins, but so mangled as to defy identification. This was not necessary, as it turned out, for the question as to whom Mr. K. had been was settled, definitely once and for all, when a frightened woman came into the little police station at Higher Wreklow and laid before Superintendent Budd certain information.

Mr. Budd later in the afternoon called to see Peter at his temporary lodgings in Higher Wicklow's one and only inn, and Peter listened stunned to the revelation that was made to him.

"George Arlington!" he gasped stupefied. "Impossible!"

The Rosebud looked at him, sadly.

"Nuthin's impossible," he murmured gently. "You'll realize that when you reach my age. And this certainly isn't. George Arlington was Mr. K. all right. His housekeeper got frightened when she found that his bed hadn't been slept in and he was nowhere to be found and came to us. We found all the information we wanted at his house. Apparently, he and Slade had been partners for months in the fencing business. So far as I can make out Arlington did the actual negotiations and Slade's job was to get rid of the stolen stuff and convert it into cash.

"If any of the people they dealt with wouldn't sell for the price they offered, or offended them in any way, Arlington tipped 'em off to the police by sending one of the 'K' letters. Everythin' would have been all right if Slade, who didn't know that 'Mr. K.' was Arlington, hadn't found out and tried a little blackmailing. I found the letter he wrote among Arlington's effects. He refused to share out the proceeds and threatened to give Arlington away—not to the police, mark you—he couldn't do that without incriminatin' himself—but to the crooks whom Arlington had squealed on. Arlington realized his danger and killed him."

"But," protested Peter, "I was with Arlington the night Slade was killed. How could he—"

"He could and he did," broke in Mr. Budd. "He killed him after you'd left." He frowned. "You walked, didn't you? Well, he rode in that fast car of his and came to 'Five Trees' by the other way. An' he had just killed Slade when Ledder turned up.

"If Arlington had known who it was, he would have probably killed him too, but he thought it was the police. You see, Slade expected Arlington that night and expected trouble. He realized that he was playing with fire, and he took the precaution of sending that letter to the Yard—he was an illiterate man—and when Arlington arrived an' started threatenin' he told him he'd sent it. What was in Slade's mind when he sent it, I can't rightly say, but I think his idea was to use it as a sort of protection, an' if things went wrong with him—and they did—that the police would arrive quickly enough to pinch the man who had killed him.

"Anyhow, Arlington cleared off, and Ledder, who had expected to find a live man, was shocked to find a dead one; so startled that he only waited long enough to take the pen and clear off."

"How did he know anything about the pen?" asked Peter.

"Andronsky and he and that feller Bilter had been working to get it for months," said Mr. Bilter. "They knew Slade kept all his money in the house and they discovered that the secret was hidden in the pen." A slow smile broke over his large face. "Slade had the last laugh, anyhow," he went on. "He must have arranged that explosive to guard his treasures and, thinkin' that Arlington might get the better of him, put false instructions in the pen to make sure that nobody 'ud benefit."

"Well, you seem to know all about it," said Peter. "How did you find all this out?"

"Partly from what I found at Arlington's, partly through what Bilter has spilt, but mostly by my own brains," retorted

194

Mr. Budd. "There's only one thing I can't quite fit in and that's how the girl comes into it. She's not very important, anyway."

*   *   *   *

It was three months later when Peter saw Mr. Budd again. He was coming out of Cook's office at Charing Cross and ran into the stout superintendent walking slowly along the pavement.

"Hello," said Mr. Budd, and eyeing the tickets in Peter's hand: "Goin' away?"

Peter nodded.

"I've got a job abroad," he said. "By the way, I think you know my wife."

Mr. Budd looked at the smiling girl who had joined them.

"I think I do," he replied. "Married, are you? Well, well, I wish I'd have known, I'd have sent you some flowers on your weddin' day."

"You're not too late now," said Peter. "We were married this morning."

THE END

Printed in Great Britain
by Amazon